When Good Men Go Bad

Book #1 of the
Men of 1302 Series

Dante D. Long

When Good Men Go Bad

Copyright © 2013 by Dante D. Long

www.darkdiamondbooks.com/author_dante.html

Dark Diamond Publishing, LLC.

Book Cover Art by Darien Pitts
Edited by Shelby Lazenby, Progressive Editing Solutions, LLC.

ISBN: 9780989578004

www.darkdiamondbooks.com

Printed in the United States of America

PUBLISHER'S NOTE
This is a work of fiction. Names, characters, places, and incidents either are the product of the author's imagination or are used factitiously, and any resemblance to actual persons, living or dead, business establishments, events, or locales is entirely coincidental.

To my beautiful children,

the reasons why I do all that I do

When Good Men Go Bad

Prologue

True friends are hard to come by. Some say that a true friend will stand by you, no matter what, while some say that true friends know each other like no other, secrets and all. This story introduces us to the three "Men of 1302" who were once college roommates that lived together in a small house near the campus of the historically black college, Pembrook College, located miles into the countryside of Arkansas. Time, trials and tribulations, individually and collectively, have strengthened the bond of these three positive men and this series looks at them, individually and collectively, as they mature and experience what life brings them.

Fate brought these three together as freshmen in the Pembrook Marching Band, also known as the High Stepping Symphony, and their lives have been intertwined since. Whether someone attended one of their wild house parties, or saw them together at an event, the three of them together turned heads. These men often complemented each other and held each other up during their days at Pembrook and will continue to do so for the rest of their lives.

With a frame of a powerful linebacker, Rodney Kirkland has the kindest heart and is quick to greet you with a hug. Sensitive and somewhat emotional, he defends what he cares about and doesn't mind using force to do so. He is definitely a walking contradiction and earned the nickname, Teflon Teddy Bear, amongst his closest friends. He is a happily married man and a new father, which has stifled his educational aspirations temporarily and inspired his hustling nature.

A musical genius is an understatement for the amount of natural talent he has in deciphering, playing and writing music. His weapons of choice are the bass guitar and tuba, though he has been known to utilize others with relative ease. As talented as he is, his desire to make a name for himself musically is overshadowed by fears of failure and lost fortunes. He has memories of his father jumping from band to band hoping to be a part of one on the way to mainstream success.

Kyle Scott is a natural born leader. Structured and oozing with common sense and foresight, he naturally steps up to leadership positions in anything that he becomes a part of. Success isn't just a desire for him, it is something that he needs. He tends to shoot down anything that just might impede that. He isn't immune to falling off the straight and narrow path, but recovering from each slip reinforces his overall determination for success.

The "country boy" from Georgia went to the Midwest and Pembrook with dreams of finding his own way. Following in his father's footsteps, Kyle is unknowingly motivated by being good enough for him and is constantly being inundated by stories of his success. Out of the three men, he is constantly the voice of reason and the peacemaker.

This novel focuses on the third of the roommates, Jasper Hooks. Some would say that he is the dreamer of the three as he sees the good in everything and feels that mostly anything is possible. He doesn't fall into your typical categories. He has a sense of envisioning what others don't see and thrives on standing out in a crowd. His out of the ordinary actions, along with his lean and muscular look, have brought him a lot of female attention over the years, wanted or not.

His conflict between his humble, carefree background and the newer pressures and stresses of the world comes to focus in the following pages. Here the transition of a young man still covered in the naivety and comforts of college begins as he is formed into manhood by ambition and disappointments, both in career and of the heart.

Chapter 1

May 11, 2002

"Let me get a little bit before we go." Jasper was giving Tina that intensely hopeful and serious look he was known for whenever the mood would hit him. Tina wasn't even looking at him as she ironed a pair of jeans, but she could hear the change in his voice as he spoke. He always bit his lower lip and deeply whispered his words when he was campaigning for some sex with her. "Naw, boo. I'm serious. Let me get a little bit before we start partying. We may be too tired or drunk later to do it."

Tina looked up at her boyfriend and calmly said, "You always want some and you are always serious." As she continued ironing, she felt him creep behind her and squeeze her ass firmly and lovingly. She spun around and laughed as she looked at a horny Jasper still biting his lower lip and rubbing himself. "Boy, we had sex earlier. You need to get ready and leave me alone. Where are you going tonight?"

Jasper, still in his boxer briefs, wasn't thinking about the many graduation parties that had already started or were about to start that night. He was only thinking about the softness that he wanted to feel on top of him and under him. "Girl, I will make it a quickie....promise." He felt like he needed to feel the wetness of her pussy and hear her love moans right then, or his night would not be right. All of the excitement of graduating from college the next day only fueled his yearning.

Tina laughed so hard that she snorted and said, "Boy, you don't ever do quickies. Really, what spots are you hitting up tonight?" She kept talking about her plans to hang out with her sorority sisters and where they were meeting up, but Jasper boldly interrupted, "Tell them you may be a lil late...aight." He wasn't usually so forceful, but he couldn't control it. His gaze was unwavering as he said, "Come here, boo. For real, come here." Submissively, Tina turned off the iron and turned around again to see him without his underwear and stroking his fully erect dick.

She grinned and tried to seem disinterested, but Jasper saw her breathing change as he knew she would soon concede to his adoring aggression. She walked out of Jasper's bedroom heading to the bathroom. She touched the doorknob and walked back in the bedroom. "You better be glad I like you, but you got 10 minutes. I ain't playing, Jasper."

42 minutes later, Jasper was panting as he hopped in the shower. His homeboy Kyle called him twice during his "quickie", and Jasper was not in the mood to hear another speech from him about being punctual. He chuckled as he overheard Tina calling

someone and say, "I'm on my way. Tell Vivian to fucking chill. I had to talk to Jasper about something real quick." After his shower, Tina rushed in to take one. She quickly got dressed, kissed Jasper on the cheek, and departed after saying to him, "Be good. I love you, ok. I will see you later."

Jasper made a similar phone call to Kyle stating that he was on his way to the local hole-in-the-wall club, The Groove, to begin their night of partying. They had an entire itinerary of house parties and clubs to stop by as they were celebrating their last night of being students. He walked downstairs and saw his roommate, Derek, sitting on the couch smiling. "Dawg, you still going to do what we talked about? You know, what you said about Tina."

Jasper dapped up his roommate and simply said, "Yep. I think it's time, bruh. I think it's time." Afterwards, he left out of the front door and said a third time, to himself, "I think it's time."

Some say that the best gift to give a mother on Mother's Day is the opportunity to hold her son's or daughter's degree from college. Pembrook College always upheld the traditional of graduating the spring semester class on Mother's Day. On May 12, 2002, Jasper Hooks was blessed to give his mom that very gift. His proud and boastful father was there, too (along with two aunts, three cousins, and some family friends), but the glow that surrounded his mother was one unlike anything he had ever seen. All of the hours spent waiting in line to register for classes each semester and the long nights of studying led to this grand culmination for Jasper, and he had deserved all the pride that he and his entourage felt.

He was just one of many in the graduating class who were in absolute awe with what was about to happen. The awe was mixed with the fatigue and alcohol that they drank merely hours ago, after a night of celebrating a future possibly enhanced by the degree that each were about to receive. The excitement while they were ushered and lined up by faculty and staff members outside the Gregory Banks Auditorium was more intoxicating than any liquor and sweeter than any chaser that could be used to cut it. Some of the future alumni of Pembrook were in tears while some were saying goodbye to old classmates and others while silently thanking God for the miracle of finally making it through. No one seemed to be contemplating anything right then but that moment.

Jasper was in line with the other soon-to-be degree holders grouped by those receiving a Bachelors in Computer Science. All students were placed alphabetically within their major, and all majors were placed in alphabetical order. He seemed just as jovial as the others, but he was lost in the upcoming future, his upcoming future. He was internally debating if he was ready to do something that many around him were not thinking about doing that day. It was time. It felt right to him, but he wondered if he was just caught up in the excitement of the moment. He visualized the good and the bad of his daunting decision as well as the vast scenarios within the gray area.

DeMarcus Allen Hunter, the guy behind Jasper and a classmate in several of his previous courses, jolted him out of his mental turmoil when he asked him to pose in a picture with him. His older brother stepped up and said, "Y'all ready? Ok, on three." The two graduates started with a serious, non-grinning pose, then swiftly and simultaneously changed facial expressions and threw up their fraternal symbols before the older brother said, "Three". DeMarcus did the symbol with his left hand and Jasper with his right. Jasper had convinced DeMarcus to join the fraternity after their junior year. They had been through a lot of good times at Pembrook, and they both felt that their roads would cross again and again over the years.

"DeMarcus, you know that I will show up at homecoming flyer than you, right?" Attending that first homecoming after graduating was a rite of passage at Pembrook, a sign that you have made it. It was common for new graduates at the following homecoming to come dressed flashier than most, even sometimes over doing it. These two would be no different.

"Bullshit! You know I have always outshined you in class, with the ladies and with the gear I sport!"

"Whatever, man! We will see, and we will let the ladies decide," Jasper said with a twisted smirk. He could already imagine the outfit he would wear and what accessories would make him stand out. He could see a scene of himself walking past a group of ladies and feeling their eyes turn with hunger as he moved slowly. He even thought that his vision was cheesy, but movies often had a scene like that.

"Ok, but not if you are still booed up with ol' girl," DeMarcus said knowing that would cease the little bout of shit-talking immediately. Jasper, wide-eyed and speechless, stopped in mid-thought.

After two hours of lining up in the heat of the early stages of another Arkansas summer, the ceremony finally began further up the road. You could tell as parents got last minute hugs and pictures or some in line started to get off of cell phones after trying to guide in late or lost family members. The line inched forward and you could hear the Pembrook Concert Band gradually getting louder and pleasantly playing a melody that wasn't quite a march but was reminiscent to melodies played at all graduations. This particular selection was different and seemed so relevant. It made one walk a little taller while subconsciously instilling a new sense of pride and purpose as if the music was written just for that year's graduates. Jasper laughed a little as he remembered the years that he played the same song for graduates before him. He was once a percussionist in both the marching and concert bands of Pembrook. Today, he felt that this song sounded special, richer, and crisper. He felt a pang of sadness as he had a quick recollection of younger, more naïve times during his coming of age adventures in the Pembrook bands.

Jasper looked around the entire place seeing the "We Love You" signs that families made expressing their joy for their graduate and the wide eyes of younger students who were either dreaming of their own graduations or already missing those senior to them as they embarked on different journeys that they one day may embark on. He scanned the auditorium to find where his parents were sitting.

Jasper's eyes finally caught his dad's wide, bearded grin and silent satisfaction which stifled any tears that his pride produced, yet kept from falling. Jasper got a little misty-eyed himself as he noticed this, but snapped back as his hometown neighbor, Ms. Juanita Clark, screamed his name louder than his parents, louder than anyone, drowning out the voices of nearby proud supporters of other graduates. Jasper waved to his parents and turned around to throw up another fraternal hand sign to his brothers seated together with his sorority sisters up in the nosebleed section. They displayed a colorful sign that stated their congratulations along with the names of the fraternal members about to walk across the stage.

It was drilled many times by the graduation committee that graduates were to walk in, "Quickly, full of distinction and in an orderly fashion," as Dr. Bernice Jones, English professor and Head of Graduation Ceremonies, had stated. It didn't stop a few energized individuals from showing out a little or screaming, "Mama!", or, "Hell yeah!" enthusiastically. One of the known big men on campus gathered a lot of attention as he looked like he was about to do a flip or something, but nervously decided against it. Dr. Jones threatened that the ceremony was going to be put on hold for such outbursts, but all knew that this joyous crowd was bound to riot if such an action truly occurred.

After the ruckus died down a little bit and all were seated, the President of Pembrook College stood up to say a few words before announcing the Dean of Religious Studies to say a prayer. The anticipation for what could be the greatest day of their lives was deeply written in the faces of the soon-to-be graduates, and this was the closing of a chapter in their lives and the opening of another one.

The Dean finished a soul-revving, and somewhat comical, prayer. He thanked the parents for birthing "the next set of

Pembrook's great marks on society" and blessed the faculty for their parts in "shaping the supple young minds to be great". The atmosphere seemed to become more invigorated as the procedures that were practiced days earlier in this same auditorium were actually going to happen. The concert band played another selection followed by the choir. Small chatter between the graduates was going on about varying subjects like how they were going to get "fucked up" later, to whom already had jobs and interviews lined up, to where the after parties were going to be. Jasper was still lost in his thoughts about his upcoming decision between the conversations he was having with those sitting near him.

After another speech by the President of Pembrook, his melodious voice sounding suddenly like famed boxing announcer Michael Buffer said, "It is finally that time. Let's all give a round of applause for the future alumni of the illustrious and historical Pembrook College!" On cue, each robed and smiling student raised to their feet. As the crowd went hysterical with cheers and clapping, Dr. Jones quickly got in to place along with the other professors who reveled in their assigned graduation day duties. Trying to keep a stern face, but looking as proud as if her own children were graduating today, Dr. Jones waited for the applause to die a little and then raised her right hand with military drill precision and held it there. As she dropped her hand with the same military sharpness and the same merrily serious face plastered on her face, the entire first row sat down with a snap, followed by each row. The audience marveled in how well executed the seating was occurring as if dominoes were falling in a timely order. As the last row sat down again, she raised the same hand sharply and the first recipients of their degrees stood up simultaneously. Instead of dropping her hand, she pointed her hand parallel to floor and the first row of students (about to receive their Master's degrees) turned suddenly to their left. She dropped her hand and executed a sharp right turn and clicked her right heel on the floor. She then walked in front of the first person in the row, stopped, clicked her right heel again, and walked toward the steps of the stage. The students walked behind her and stopped at the top step, and Dr. Jones proceeded to walk to her spot on the stage which was after the president and before the guest speaker.

You could still see the shocked expressions of those people in the stadium seating who have never seen such refined and ritualistic happenings at a graduation. The Pembrook staff designated as ushers manned their positions with delight as they waited to give the proper cues to each succeeding row as names were called and students transformed into alumni by walking across the stage, shaking hands with each party on stage, and receiving an empty diploma cover embossed with the school's coat of arms in gold ink. Actual degrees would be received in designated rooms after the ceremony to prevent anyone from receiving a misplaced one. Row after row, the first section received their Master's degrees. There was a small transition in which Dr. Jones again did the same ritual with those due to receive their Bachelor's degree. The crowd seemed to be in just as much admiration the second time as the first as family members, students and well-wishers were starting to holler out the names of their loved one and friends.

As he sat there anxiously waiting for his row to stand up and his name to be eventually called, Jasper looked up at his parents, then over to his boo, Tina, a few rows ahead of him. She just happened to be smiling back at him as their eyes met. Her row just sat down with their diploma holders in hand after their names were called, and they walked across that red stage with all the school's key leaders and staff draped in varying colorful robes with even more varying tassels and stoles. He knew that it was so right for him to want to marry that girl, and he started to accept the fact, right then, that he actually asked her to move with him back to Memphis only weeks prior. He was looking forward to starting his career at InfoTech Solutions Incorporated and his life with Tina. He again was playing his mental film of how he thought she would act when he called a toast later in front of his friends and family, asked her to join him and proposed to her. He knew it was not typical to propose without a ring, but he knew that most would understand since he was in the midst of becoming a career man after spending most of his money paying tuition all the years prior. Tina was oblivious to her boyfriend's thoughts as he waved and smiled back.

Time seemed to slow down as Jasper's row was called. Flashbacks of the good times and bad times during his duration at Pembrook flowed through his mind. The frat parties, the study groups, the various girls and flings, the band trips, the accomplishments and the disappointments.....they all seemed to fast forward in his mind suddenly. He could hear his own heartbeat drowning out the noise from the attendees and feel the beads of sweat forming on his forehead and under his arms as his row began their ascent up the stairs of the stage. He turned his head for a final nod toward his parents and waited for his name to be called.

As he heard his name called, the noises from the audience escalated to higher levels. This was partly his family's group cheering, but mostly from the many friends, admirers, and fans that he acquired over the years. Jasper was not the most popular man on campus, but he gained a lot of attention that warranted many to know his name, whether it was through his former escapades in the band, or by participating in fraternity activities like step shows. At a small school like Pembrook, it was not hard to be known, whether a good or bad reputation followed your name. Jasper was one of those who would be known and remembered with an overall good reputation. He silently regarded this and could hear his father asking him later, "Boy, what was all that commotion about when they called your name?"

A few others did a little celebratory walk or gesture at the end of the walk across the stage. Jasper planned on not being one of those people, but a feeling amped up by the commotion that followed his name, surged into him like someone touching a striped, live electrical wire. As he neared the end of the stage, he, without thinking, looked up toward the area where his family sat and pointed, then turned toward the group of fraternally associated acquaintances, paused, and posed with his fraternity's hand sign. Some of those who noticed, cheered loudly again before he exited the stage.

Chapter 2

Jasper was parting the sea of graduation robes and the proud supporters to get to his family who were waiting across the street by a large oak tree as decided earlier that morning in order to easily be found. He hugged a few classmates on the way, gave some dap to others, and posed for a few pictures before actually making it there. He was surprised to see Tina and her family there as well. He showed nothing but teeth as he hugged his dad, his mom, and everyone else that made the road trip to see him. Memphis was only 40 minutes away, but everyone was not going to make that drive, especially on a Sunday. He was grateful for those who did and were there to celebrate his day. He was anxious to see who would be around to offer their congratulations later.

Impervious to the presence of his parents and Tina's, Jasper walked right up to Tina, hugged her, and planted a passionate, desire–filled kiss on the lips that he loved so genuinely. "Congrats baby!" came from his own as he noticed that she was probably more embarrassed than his mom. "Congrats to you, too," she said with a loving look that could be seen in the face of a woman married to the perfect man for 20 years, rather than one of a woman that has dated a man off and on for just two years.

Tina's mom broke up the gentle moment by saying, "You two should pose for a picture together." Jasper looked up to see a mixture of shock, yet understanding and embarrassment on the faces of those around him. Out of the corner of his eye, he noticed Tara, one of his former flings during one of the times that he and Tina were apart, paying attention as well. He did not regard Tara's look as he posed with his two favorite girls, Tina and his mom.

The group temporarily separated so the two brand new alumni could go and pick up their actual diplomas. They had agreed to meet up by the statue of Jeremiah Pembrook, who was founder of the city of Pembrook, in about thirty minutes. Jasper gave plenty of hugs and hi-fives as he journeyed toward the Jeffrey A. Riley Building where most computer science majors spent their days and nights. The name of the building was recently changed to honor a great inventor that graduated from Pembrook years ago and gave unwavering support to the school until his death in 1985.

On his way, he even stopped to pose with Tara in a picture. Tara was a junior at Pembrook, so it was not her graduation day. She just had to get one more hug from him because she would truly miss him, though their last sexual encounter was six months ago. She went where she knew Jasper would go and Tina wouldn't right then which was in front of the building where they had met in the hallways between classes a year and a half ago, where today he was going to pick up his actual diploma. During their hug, she whispered, "God knows that I am going to miss you!" Jasper could feel himself getting hard as he reminisced how that caramel ass looked so perfect in the moonlight the last time they were together. The contrast of her fair skin and his dark, smooth chocolate skin intertwined together brought him to almost full erection as he pushed her back. He broke her heart that last time for he knew it was their last moonlit dance when he opened the door that night. He told her that he was thinking about going back to Tina before the first candle was lit that night. Just a little bit, he would miss her too. She was part of his past, and today was the beginning of a whole new future. Jasper gave her a little peck on the cheek and turned around without looking back as he ascended the steps of his destination.

With the distraction of Tara out of the way, he walked into the building and into a large classroom that most of the buildings student inhabitants used after hours to cram for exams or collaborate with others. He stood in line and saw DeMarcus Hunter walk in.

"After I have dinner with my folks, I'ma come through to kick it with you and the old folks," DeMarcus said as he walked up to Jasper.

Jasper replied back, "Ok, we are going to kick it all night, so we will be there until whenever. I can't promise that any food will be left, but it's whatever. Tell all the bruhs that you see."

"I saw Tara outside looking like she wanted to come too," DeMarcus exclaimed with a devilish grin.

Jasper snapped back, "Motherfucka, don't play with me! I better not see her there. I ain't playing with you!"

The gruff in his voice caused DeMarcus to blink as he jerked his head back and said, "My bad! Just playing with you, frat." DeMarcus went to the back of the line and was thinking that if Jasper really was truly over her, he might not be mad if he took a stab at her. By stab, he really was thinking of how many ways he would want to poke a beautiful thing like that with the part of his body designed for poking.

After receiving the sacred document and a few more hugs, brief conversations, and phone number exchanges, Jasper reached for the keys to his new car and walked toward the distant parking lot. Parking that morning was definitely crazy so he had to park wherever he could, and not really giving a damn about the ticket that may be on his windshield. Luckily, there wasn't one. The car wasn't actually brand new, but his 1999 gold-colored Honda Civic was new to him. It was a graduation gift given to Jasper by his father a month prior. It replaced the 1982 Ford Escort he'd had since his sophomore year.

He finally was on his way to meet his folks at the statue. He was shocked to find a nearby parking spot since he figured every graduate would want to take a picture in their cap and gown at the statue with proud friends and family. He cracked the front windows, turned off the ignition and checked his text messages on his phone, knowing that his folks were waiting on him, and he was a little late. The list of received messages was mostly congratulatory; one was from Tara, some were from various frat brothers and sorority sisters asking about his graduation party or wanting to take pictures on the yard where the organization's historical area was. His mom had sent a text asking him to hurry his slow ass up.

He answered a few back, giving his address to those who didn't have it or simply saying "Thanks". While he typed a text to his frat brother Charles, Tina knocked on the window. Jasper looked up and his breath stopped a second as he could only focus on her lips and the mulberry shade of lipstick that she was wearing. As he got out of the car, she asked him what was taking him so long and stated that her mom was getting restless. Jasper rolled his eyes and whispered in her ear, "So umm…you know what I wanna do before we hit the road, right?" Tina blushed and said "Come on, boy. Let's take these pictures."

He had started sweating under the dark robe as he walked across the well-manicured square, lined with benches and several symbolic statues, along the path to the enormous statue of Pembrook's founder. A few families and new alumni were still waiting to take pictures. The rush was over since Jasper took his "sweet time", as his mom would say, getting to the area. Ms. Jackson, Tina's mom, did look a little perturbed, and Mr. Jackson was grinning with his usual goofy, relaxed look. Jasper arrogantly looked at everyone as the pride of the day, his day, had started to sink in, as he looked at his parents again and those with them. His mom looked like half of her wanted to say, "What the hell is wrong with you making us wait in this damn, hot sun?", and the other half just wanting to kiss and hug her only son.

Jasper held up the diploma cover and handed it to his mom who shrieked with ear-piercing joy as she grabbed it and said "Thank you baby," as if he was giving it to her. He then grabbed her and said, as if in a hurry, "Let's take these pictures." Tina was thinking the same thing that he was, which was to get the pictures out of the way so they could separately get to the campus yard to do the traditional singing of songs and chants that most fraternities and sororities did after special occasions and gatherings like graduation. She rubbed on her red and white stole embroidered with the letters of her sorority in anticipation to do differently what she had done years prior. Now it was her turn to be in the inner circle receiving the praises and love instead of being on the outside circle singing to the big sisters. Jasper was wondering if the shoes he wore were going to be comfortable enough to do a few step routines with his frat brothers, though he knew he would participate even if he was barefooted.

One by one, everyone posed for individual pictures by the statue, then pictures with Jasper or Tina, then pictures with both. After ten minutes, both Tina and Jasper were getting impatient. They were almost ready to cut the special moment to a close in order to get to their respective groups. Tina's mom came to the rescue, sort of, by letting out a loud sigh and purposely saying to her husband, "Terrence, it is sooooo hot out here in this sun!" Everyone got the hint (and Ms. Hooks stifled a comment), and gathered for one last picture. The moment still seemed surreal even if Ms. Jackson wanted to be in another place.

The two lovebirds, now alumni of Pembrook College, pulled their parents to separate sides of the grassy area surrounding the statue to have a little palaver before they decided to hit the road. Mr. and Ms. Hooks were merry and discussing how everything was laid out for the night's graduation party back in Memphis. Jasper's mom said with a sweet, yet stern tone, since she knew that he was usually late, "What time are you going to be there, baby?" On the other end, Tina was begging her parents not to embarrass her tonight at the home of her lover. Mr. Jackson had no words. He was ready to hang out with the parents of the one who might be his son-in-law one day, hopefully. The vocal one, his wife, was still trying to convince her daughter that she was tired and wanted to only have dinner in Memphis and catch a flight the next day. It seemed like the equally vocal Ms. Hooks could either hear what Ms. Jackson was saying or could assume what she was saying. They suddenly and silently regarded each other as if they read each other's thoughts. Eerily, they both stopped talking and felt the urge to leave.

After a few more minutes, the group started to dissipate and walk to their cars. The Hooks had a party to host. Ms. Jackson needed a nap. The high temperature of the day started to subside, but definitely wasn't gone. There was more celebrating to do, more futures to talk about, and more moving on to the next phase of life to do. The Hooks started the journey back to Memphis toward the Hernando DeSoto Bridge.

Jasper and Tina walked rather quickly down University Avenue to the "Yard", which was the large grass area by the School of Business building and favorite hangout of most of the Pembrook students. The members of their organizations were still around as if waiting for them to join them for more pictures and the singing of songs and hymns. A crowd of onlookers started to gather around the trees and benches that were usually occupied by members of Jasper's fraternity awaiting a show. Jasper's heart started to race again since he knew that it was showtime.

Before their parents were out of the city limits toward Memphis, Tina cried as she hugged various sorority sisters after they handed her a bouquet of red and white roses. Jasper hopped around with other members of his fraternity in a mini step show as the crowd took pictures. Jasper invited others to join him in Memphis after soaking his shirt with sweat after stepping for twenty minutes. His enthusiasm was still soaring as he noticed Tina walking toward the crowd with that my-feet-hurt-so-let's-go look.

After saying goodbye to their parents and friends, both Tina and Jasper headed back to his place. Tina already had some stuff packed at his apartment since she had been staying there pretty regularly. Tina prepared to take a shower as Jasper drank three glasses of water and gathered some clothes for the short stay at his parents' house. She playfully fought off his advances after a few minutes of hugging and kissing in his bedroom. Jasper's roommate was not home, and he wanted to take advantage of that fact as well as his euphoria from the day's activities and what was to come that night.

The energy in Jasper was soaring with yearning. He felt that he would explode just from the little fooling around that they did. He reluctantly backed off so Tina could get a shower in before they hit the road, but he wanted to release some of the growing anticipation in him. He wanted to ignite again some of the deep desire that steadily had been growing for the one who he would call fiancé in mere hours. He half-mindedly packed some clothes and necessities as he listened for the shower to be turned off. He had already unlocked the door with a hanger while she was in the shower. After a few minutes, he rushed in the bathroom definitely startling his "boo" with a hungry, determined look in his eyes. Even with no makeup and wearing only a shower cap, she looked extremely stunning.

She already knew what that look meant as she gazed back at him with her heart still racing from the sudden entry. She mentally complained to herself about having to take another shower as she dropped the towel and snatched off her shower cap merely seconds before Jasper firmly, yet lovingly held her against the wall while kissing her still damp body. She was in a lustful awe as she thought of how much she loved his spontaneity and did not resist his lips, his tongue, and his hands. It didn't matter if Jasper's roommate Derek would have come home that very second. The moment was so intense that it couldn't be stopped.

Jasper whispered, "I love you", a couple of times as he stepped back to grab a condom out of his pocket. Even when struck by lust, he never lost his sense about protection. He guided her to the sink and dropped his pants while standing behind her. He looked at the beautiful eyes staring back at him in the mirror as he rolled on the Trojan condom. He then playfully smacked her ass before he entered her from behind. Neither one cared that the bathroom door was wide open and Derek's whereabouts were unknown as they sexually celebrated their graduation and feelings for each other. She held on the counter with one hand and the other one on the wall while Jasper powerfully pleased her. Her head almost hit the mirror several times as her knees grew wobbly from the gratification and force coming from Jasper's thrust. After several minutes, he led her by her hand to his bedroom to continue the passionate and powerful session. This time he remembered to close the door.

A while later, after an almost aerobic bout of sex and a short nap, the two lovers individually took their showers, changed clothes, and packed their cars for the trek to Memphis and the awaiting graduation party. They both called their parents to let them know that they were on their way. Jasper made a few other calls to ensure that the liquor was in place and that his best friends Kyle and Rodney were coming. Before they pulled off, he ran back into the apartment to grab a CD that he had made the night before.

Chapter 3

After a small trip, mostly consisting of two-lane country roads before hitting a major highway, Tina arrived at the residence of the Hooks, followed shortly by Jasper. Several supporters and associates were already full and at different levels of intoxication, but the essence of the event was magnetic. More hugs and gifts greeted Jasper as he made his way toward the back of the house to greet his parents. He wanted to make a plate as well as fill a cup with a beverage as well. He introduced Tina to those that did not know her along the way.

The old school hit "Gigolos Get Lonely Too" by Morris Day and the Time was softly playing on a stereo moved to the back porch as the couple entered the backyard to eat and fellowship. Jasper had an overloaded plate with his mom's best soul food and a Dixie cup with his favorite type of vodka and cranberry juice. Tina followed him like a shadow, after trying to get her parents to join them outside where most of the guests were hanging. She had a filled plate of food as well, but her Dixie cup was minus the alcohol. She never drank around her parents despite her legal ability to do so.

Tina's family was definitely well to do. Both of her parents were successful dentists in New York. Though the Hooks household was certainly in a nice middle-class neighborhood in Whitehaven (a subdivision of Memphis) and well taken care of, you could see the slight discomfort that Tina's mom felt. She sat on a sofa in the living room barely talking and seemed as if she wanted to leave as soon as possible. Tina noticed and tried to cover for her mother's seemingly stuck-up countenance by saying that she was just tired from the flight. Tina was so disgusted and discomfited that her mom would act this way. She was somewhat baffled that her dad had dealt with it for so many years.

Eventually, Mr. Jackson had enough of trying to appease his wife and decided to join the congregation of down-to-earth people in the back. After a few minutes alone on the sofa, Ms. Jackson, looking like a jeweled poodle that just got its tail stepped on, eventually followed suit, fake smile and all. As she walked up to her husband, she overheard him saying to Tina, "So baby girl, what is next? I know we talked about it some, but what's in the plans for you? Did you think about what I told you last month?"

Jasper stepped up, before Tina could look her dad in the eyes, and he said, "We have been looking for her some employment near my job, but she may have to work in Cordova or Collierville." The frown now planted on her father's face spoke volumes. Jasper looked at his girlfriend and said, "I thought that you told him." He could see Ms. Jackson creeping up behind him with her mouth open, unable to speak. "Ooooh shit," was whispered from Jasper's lips a little more audible then what he wanted, but he realized the storm that was about to form at this time of celebration and looked toward the ground to hide his expression of anger and disappointment in his girlfriend. She swore that she discussed this with her parents and that they supported it with a few reservations. He knew then that the subject might not have come up at all prior to that moment.

Tina precipitously grabbed her mom by the hand and pulled her away to talk. She felt an embarrassing confrontation about to occur in front of all of those people. "Mommy, remember I told you that I wanted to stay down south, right?"

Ms. Jackson finally closed her mouth and quickly reopened it to say, "I thought you wanted to spend the rest of the summer in Arkansas before beginning your life in New York." The way that she said some of those words really irritated Tina.

"What is up with this getting a job in Cordova? So I guess that you plan to shack up with him too?" Ms. Jackson was belligerent as she said that and pointed at Jasper in a condescending manner. Jasper glared up at Tina, then her mom and almost said, "What the fuck does that mean?", before noticing his dad putting his cup down and walking toward them.

Mr. Hooks noticed a shift in the mood of his only son and was going to be *goddamned* if these *uppity New Yorkers* were going to come down to his house and *start some shit*. That is one thing that Jeffrey Hooks would not stand for….any unruly guests at his house, especially today. He felt that Mr. Jackson was okay to converse with and that he might have just lost his sense of where he came from at some point. Regardless, he was about to shut down his wife since he wasn't about to do it. Tina continued to pull at her mom as the other guests started to whisper. Most of them already knew what the Jacksons were just finding out.

Jasper's head started to spin with confusion, anger, doubt, and a plethora of other feelings. Was he to get involved in this family squabble, and should he stand up for himself and his lady? Playing what to say in his head, he had a sudden, comical vision of a younger Mr. Jackson standing before him mean mugging him with a white t-shirt and some Timberland boots (as some of the young students at Pembrook from New York wore regardless of the season) and held back a smile. It seemed that the accent of the New Yorkers got thicker as they got angry, and it was no different for Mr. Terrence Jackson, regardless of how refined he had become over the years.

Further in the back yard, Tina was almost in tears as she pleaded to her mom to understand. Originally, she planned on staying around Pembrook to be a professor's assistant but now felt like moving to Memphis would be best to jump start her own career and be closer to the man that she loved. Her mom talked about marriage and all of the strings she had to pull to open up some doors for Tina in New York. The crowd at the party was mixed with nosey onlookers and those who didn't care, other than that the mood of the party was dampened.

The patriarchs of the newly graduated lovers were locked in an overly masculine, yet mature talk about being grown, making mistakes and staying out of it. Jasper interjected how he felt about Tina, that he loved her, and that he already had a job lined up. It took every ounce of social etiquette in her, but Ms. Hooks just smiled and ensured the other guests that everything was ok while encouraging all to disregard the little commotion taking place. Just when it seemed that things were going to take a turn for the worst, Rodney and Kyle showed up and made their presence known with Kyle screaming, "We up in here!! What's up everybody?" Little did they know that they walked into a dispute between lovers and families, and it seemed that all parties involved silenced at once. Rodney and Kyle oddly seemed to have an overwhelming effect on a crowd, especially when they showed up somewhere with Jasper at the same time.

The interruption was perfectly timed, and Jasper was visibly thankful. He could always count on his two good friends, and this time was no different, even though it wasn't planned. The two fathers looked at each other with a silent understanding to either discuss this later or not at all. Mr. Jackson said a few wise words, shushing his wife immediately before she could say something, and gave an apprehensive consent to Jasper. Ms. Jackson most definitely wasn't happy or through talking, but she realized as she calmed down the scene they might have made and proceeded to plaster her face with a replica of a smile, which she was typically known to do. Seeing this, Jasper walked past them to greet his homeboys.

Chapter 4

Jasper excitedly said, "Boy, am I happy to see y'all up in here!" He said the words "up in here" the same way that Kyle said it. Rodney was always happy to see his homeboy, but was visibly deep in thought. Though he was at a graduation celebration, he really wasn't in the mood for it, since this should have been his graduation as well. He dropped out of school the year prior to support his new wife and infant daughter. Kyle graduated today along with Jasper and he could sense the thoughts of his friend. He could only imagine what was going through his head and was not going to bring it up unless it was brought up to him.

The other guests started back up with their partying and socializing since the family feud was now over. The sound of dominoes slapping and people talking shit was just as loud as before. The Jacksons were talking in the front yard, and no one missed their presence in the backyard....not even Tina. Kyle and Rodney both had a beer in their hands as they grabbed the silent leader of their group, Jasper, and went to the side of the house to talk. Mr. Hooks almost followed them but chose to check on the meat still on his grill.

"Soooo....what the hell just happened?" said Kyle before taking a sip of his beer. Rodney followed with, "Pimp, I thought that you were about to slap somebody, or your dad was about to go old school and shank somebody. No one messes with Daddy J. Hooks!"

Jasper had started to calm down, but still had a somewhat contorted look on his face as he laughed and replied, "The Jacksons didn't want any mess up in here. I thought that Tina fucking told them though. I can't believe that shit came out here! Tonight was supposed to be so much different, man....so much different."

Rodney jumped in, "You are probably wondering if you can trust her, huh? Wondering if she lied about some other stuff, huh, pimp? I wouldn't sweat that shit, na-mean? You see how difficult her parents be acting and shit." Jasper marveled at the way that Rodney always kept it real with him, even at a time like this.

Always the more rational one of the trio, Kyle looked Jasper in the eye and stated, "Bruh, maybe you should wait on your lil announcement. Hell, I was hoping that you didn't do it before we got here." Jasper's look became suddenly somber and his shoulders slumped as he accepted what he already knew to be true; maybe he should wait to propose to Tina. He didn't have a ring yet anyway.

Rodney chimed in with, "Man, do what you feel…just do it when you are ready and you feel that it is right. I don't regret marriage, but I knew that it was right….na-mean."

"I agree with your friends, but it is your choice." Jeffrey Hooks caught the end of the young men's conversation. "I know that you want to add to the excitement of your graduation," Rodney subconsciously looked down, "but trust your ol' dad, you should wait until all this clears up." He hugged his son, and patted Rodney on the shoulder. As he walked away, he said over his shoulder, "You know that uppity New Yorker didn't want to get a southern ass whooping." The three buddies erupted in laughter and headed back to the back of the house.

An hour later, the fire of the grill was reduced to a glow among the ashes, the liquor bottles were almost empty as bellies were full, and everyone was having a good time. Even Ms. Jackson enjoyed talking with some of the older women that were attendees. Mr. Jackson became more of that younger picture Jasper had envisioned as he swallowed bottles of beer and joined Mr. Hooks in playing Spades with Jasper's frat brothers, Eric and Antonio. Earlier, he handed his wife the car keys because he knew that she was going to have to drive them back to the hotel despite the fact that she didn't want to.

Tina had avoided her lover for a while until Ms. Hooks offered some womanly advice to the embarrassed and withdrawn young lady. "Jasper stood up to us when he wanted to learn how to drive. Against our wishes, he saved up his money and paid for his own lessons to show us that he was capable of handling it. We honestly were more scared that our little boy was growing up too fast and wouldn't need us anymore. He hasn't had a ticket yet. Baby, what I am saying is that you may need to teach yourself how to drive. Your parents love you, but you control your destiny." Tina could see the point that Ms. Hooks was making.

Jasper walked up behind Tina shortly after his mom walked away. Liquor and time helped to sober up the anger that he felt earlier. For him, it was a good day despite the little spat they had in the backyard. He attempted to look into her eyes, and she couldn't even raise her head to meet his gaze. Though others were looking, Jasper lifted her chin and kissed her cheek before moving to her lips, gaze unchanging. He felt forgiveness, love, lust, and some sense of duty to his girlfriend. He knew that he had to seize that moment. There was an overwhelming feeling that all felt right.

It is funny how sometimes those close to you know you better than you know yourself. Kyle felt a change in the air as if some strange aroma slapped his nose. He knew that Jasper was about to make a mistake, and that he had to do something about it….for his own good. He started to purposely cut his conversation short with a young lady that he met at the Hooks home with the intention of grabbing Jasper's attention with a lame joke or something. His head pounded with thoughts of *Oh shit, he is about to propose*, and *Not now, not now*. The trance that his former roommate and forever best friend was in was too focused, too full of meaning. His heart raced as if he had the power to stop a train wreck like a caped superhero, and as he excused himself from the woman he was talking to, Jasper looked up and announced, "Everyone, can I have your attention?" Too late.

All eyes were on the man of the hour, but all were not happy. It was obvious to most people in the room, except for Tina, what was about to go down. Ms. Jackson stood up and Kyle stopped in his tracks. Rodney took a big gulp of his drink while Mr. Hooks almost knocked over his. Jasper decided against playing the special CD that he made for that moment and nervously continued. "I would like to thank everyone for coming out tonight and having a good time. Today was a good day. To make it even better, I would like to say a few words." Ms. Jackson sat back down thinking that maybe she wouldn't be a mother-in-law yet. Jasper continued with, "A chapter of my life closed when I walked across that stage, and it is time to open up another." He kneeled on his left knee as gasps and whispers were heard.

He lovingly looked at Tina and said, "Baby, we have been through a lot, but I want you to be there with me to go through a lot more. I love you, and I want you to marry me." Before she could answer, he continued, "I know that I don't have a ring yet, but I plan to change that shortly."

Tina felt like she was about to faint, but not as much as her mother. She finally remembered to breathe and finally looked Jasper in the eye. She paused a little longer and said, "Yes, baby. I love you." There were some "awwws" and clapping, but the people closest to those two were all speechless, lost in a compilation of happiness and a feeling of cautious hopefulness. Mr. Jackson was visibly torn in his emotions while trying to keep his wife from blurting out a comment. He eyed where his suit jacket and keys were because he knew that they would have to leave soon.

The two lovers were vanished in their union and were smiling and whispering to each other. Kyle didn't move until Rodney tapped him on the shoulder, "It's ok, bruh. They will be fine." Kyle felt happy for his homeboy but felt a certain burden in that he hoped that he wasn't too late to stop a massive mistake. Only time would tell.

Mr. Hooks, always wise and observant, had to spin out of his shock and drop a few positive words to shake up those that were naysayers and still suffering from slight shock. He walked up to his son and Tina and grabbed their hands. He looked proud and paternal at both of them and stated, "Congratulations you two. May God smile on your love and your future success. Always remember that marriage takes work…more work than you had to do for your degrees." You could hear a few "Amen!" and "Alright!" comments among the guests. "I know that you both will do fine as long as you keep the Lord first in your life and keep the lines of communication open." He looked toward his wife, smiled, and cracked a joke, "That is how I stayed married to my lovely Delphina all of these years. I think I lost some of my hearing for all the listening I had to do. Ha, ha!"

The mood was lightened some, and people started walking up to hug and congratulate the couple. It was late, and some started to say their goodbyes as well. Ms. Hooks walked over to the Jacksons with somewhat of a peace offering. "It is on us to help guide them. We knew this day would possibly come. They will be fine, and I ask that you support your daughter right now." She looked directly at the matron of the Jackson family intently as she stated that last sentence. Her look was returned with one of slight disgust and intimidation. Mr. Jackson instantly popped up and walked toward his daughter. He stopped after a few steps and looked firmly at his wife as if saying, *Baby, get your ass up!* She complied and joined her husband. Jasper saw the whole thing and thought about what he would have to deal with as they would be his future in-laws.

Tyrone Pettiway, a junior at Pembrook, had just said goodbye to his former classmates as the Jacksons walked up. Mr. Jackson sincerely congratulated the two and hugged his daughter. However, the fakeness of his wife was sickening though as she smiled and hugged Jasper, then her daughter. Tina and her fiancé kept their comments to themselves. Her parents told her that they had a good time and were about to go to the hotel to get ready for tomorrow. They offered to take the couple to lunch before they flew back to New York. Tina smiled, but could only imagine the argument that they were going to have on the way back to the Peabody Hotel.

Mr. Jackson said goodbye to Mr. Hooks with a firm handshake and a slight slur in his voice. "Jeffrey, I haven't partied like that in years! I thank you for your hospitality and the good food. We have to get some rest before we fly out tomorrow. We will talk Tuesday." It was obvious what that talk would be about. The mothers started to clean up a little bit as they talked. The understanding between them was clear; they would never be friends, but now was not the time to be enemies. There was no trust between them, and they both loved their children.

After the final guests left and the house was converted back to a home, the three friends that once stayed at 1302 Austin Street in Pembrook, Arkansas remained in the backyard talking and drinking a little bit of what was left from the celebration. The Hooks had been up way past their bedtime and choose to let them be as the sun was due to rise in mere hours. Tina was already sleeping in one of the guest bedrooms. Jasper's mother made sure to state to her in front of Jasper, "You may be engaged, but not married, yet. I better not wake up and see that door locked with Jasper lying up in there." Tina understood.

The young men with the whole world in front of them talked about that night, disagreed about scenarios of the past, and talked about their various futures. Kyle was just commissioned in the Army as a Second Lieutenant and was just waiting for his initial training course date for his career designation. Rodney was going back to Pembrook to continue to work, focus on getting back in school, and take care of his new family. "Man, you know Katrina is going to trip about letting me hang out this long, and I got to meet up with some people who want to start a band when I get back." Rodney stated all of that drowsily and drained from exhausting manual labor just to make ends meet and his consumption of alcoholic beverages.

Jasper was changing channels in his mind. He was flipping between his upcoming job, his engagement to Tina, all the other things that transpired that night, and a bunch of other stuff. He even thought about Tara for a few minutes. Some women just leave an impression on you that is hard to shake. Tara was that one for Jasper. She was part of his past now, and though the guys joked about him missing her, he knew there was no future…at all.

As the sun slowly started to make its presence known, the guys laid in different spots in the living room. The conversation flipped to a friendly and jokingly intense discussion about whose fraternity was the best. It amazed a lot of the students at Pembrook how these three guys could still be such good friends though all were in different social fraternities. Words like "ashy"," punk", and "lame" filled the air at a volume that almost made Delphina Hooks get out of her bed twice to shush them. All three would have a bond that no other social or fraternal order could separate….ever.

Chapter 5

The next day began how many days did in the past. Ms. Hooks was in the kitchen cooking for her sons, one actual and two adopted. Her husband was in the backyard separating beer and soda cans from beer bottles in the back and cleaning his large pit grill. Slowly, the guys woke up one by one and joined Tina who was helping her future mother-in-law prepare the meal. It was clearly a chance for her to talk with Ms. Hooks and get some extra brownie points. It was also hard to ignore the glow that seemed to gleam around Tina. The somewhat sheltering world of college only gave Tina and the three former roommates the beginning of adult troubles and triumphs, but that day Tina felt grown and ready for the world. Her dreams the night prior were filled with Barbie doll fantasies of having the perfect man, the perfect job, and the perfect life.

Rodney arrived in the kitchen first. Being the biggest of the three guys, he had no shame when it came to food. His saying was, "Hell, when you get hungry, eat. Simple!" He washed up and sat at the table anticipating the food, whose smell woke him up that morning. He grabbed a plate, said grace, and started eating without waiting on his homeboys. He also knew that he had to get back home sooner than later. His wife, Katrina, had given him a pass to hang out which was rare, and he didn't want to ruin his chance for a new one. He pulled out his phone to send her a quick text before he got too deep into his plate.

Kyle was next to hit the kitchen with thoughts of soaking up the liquid libations that were still present in his body and rehydrating as well. He laughed as he tapped Rodney in the back of the head and was met with, "Good morning, pimp! I got to eat, and I got to go." He understood. He then took a moment to look at Tina with thoughts of what happened the night before. He thought of Katrina, Rodney, and their young marriage and wondered if Tina and Jasper would really work out. If the incidents the night before were any indication, it made him nervous. He always knew that he would be the last of the three buddies to get married, but he wished that Jasper would wait. That is how Jasper was to him: headstrong, impatient, and a sucker for love.

As if Tina could feel the thoughts of Kyle hitting her in the back of the head, she turned to face him and thought she saw a smirk disappear from his face. She ignored her urge to say something because it would not be proper to do it in front of her future mother-in-law. She never understood why Kyle always had something against her, but that didn't matter anymore. He would just have to get over it because she was not going anywhere. He looked at her daringly, as if he wanted her to know that he really did have a problem with her and the new engagement. Rodney looked up from his plate, noticed the tension, and continued to eat his food as if nothing happened.

Just then, Jasper came into the kitchen asking where his dad was. "Boy, get your rusty behind upstairs and clean yourself up. Your friends know better than you, and I didn't raise them!" screamed Ms. Hooks. Rodney grabbed another plate of food as Tina did the same without speaking. Jasper walked over to his fiancé and grabbed her from behind with a strong hug.

"Boy, I ain't playing with you, get out of my damn kitchen and get cleaned up. Your boo will be here when you get back." Ms. Hooks waved her hands in a big circle as she said "boo", mocking how the young ladies at her job said it when they talked about their latest flings and one-night stands in the break room.

Upon Jasper's return, all of the favorite people in his life were eating and laughing about how some guests were acting the prior night. He grabbed a plate, scooped up whatever food was left and joined in the conversation. The mood was full of love and cheerful communication led by the patriarch of the Hook clan at the head of the table.

Shortly after breakfast, Mr. Hooks returned back to his bed to sleep. Rodney called his wife and said, "Good morning, lil angel," to his daughter before getting back on the road to Pembrook. His life was not yet that of a graduate. He had to return to work after taking two days off to enjoy the festivities with his homeboys. The shame that he felt deep down was overshadowed by optimism. He knew that God's divine plan took his life down another path in which graduation was not in his current timeline, but it would be…no doubt.

Kyle gathered his things, said his goodbyes, and went to hang out with his parents before they flew home to Georgia. "Mama" Hooks went upstairs shortly after that, leaving the two lovebirds to talk and get the alone time that both craved all morning. Jasper waited until his parent's bedroom door closed and ran over to Tina kissing her with deep intensity, almost ready to repeat the activity that transpired in his bathroom the day before. Tina slapped his hand away.

"J, what the hell's wrong with you? Your mom is going to think that I am a hoe! Stop that."

They went to the backyard to talk about college, future plans, and wedding ideas. Love and excitement was quite evident in their gestures and conversation, as well as their kisses in the warmth of the humid Memphis summer. The mood was interrupted by a phone call to Tina's cell phone, which was quietly charging by the kitchen sink. "Baby, I got to go," were her words after a brief talk with her mom. She packed up her stuff and received a few pinches and kisses along the way from Jasper. After one last adoring kiss, she walked to her car, rushing to get to her parents for a late lunch. "Tell your dad and mom that I said thanks for their hospitality, baby. I will call you later." As Jasper watched her walk to her car parked on the side street, he was thinking about seeing her walk in a wedding dress. He subconsciously grabbed his shorts with excitement. He chuckled and closed the door still swimming in his warm and fuzzy moment.

Two weeks later, life returned to normal for the most part for the city of Pembrook with all of the expected changes after a graduation. Some of those who were still students at the college enjoyed the break before summer school. Most of the new alumni were packing up and leaving the place of higher education, where lives were changed and memories were formed. The bittersweet feeling among them was evident as some tried to get in their last few college parties before leaving, while moving trucks and packed up cars were seen all over the city.

Nothing really changed for Rodney as he returned to his routine of family life and constantly working. The audition that he had for a local band went well, and he was called back to be the bass guitarist. The talent that he possessed musically was extraordinary, and he welcomed any opportunity to showcase his skills and share that gift with the world. His nights were crammed with thoughts of how he would balance his responsibilities and everyday life with his desire to play and write music while never forgetting the ultimate goal of becoming an alumnus of Pembrook as well.

Kyle had departed Pembrook days after graduation and went back to his hometown of Atlanta, Georgia. He was enjoying his time with his childhood friends and family before his ordered date to sign in to Fort Leonard Wood, Missouri to attend his officer basic course, which was sooner then he wanted. After the events of September 11, 2001, the military as a whole changed, especially the Army. His commission as a Second Lieutenant brought about much pride and patriotism in him, as well as a lot of uncertainty. The Army was no longer just a 9-to-5 job anymore. The possibility of deploying to Iraq was always looming in the minds of all soldiers and officers, new or old, from West Point to Pembrook.

Jasper was making moves in his post-collegiate life as well. He had one more week left on his job at a supermarket in a small town near Pembrook. His new job awaited him in Memphis as a Network Test Engineer/Helpdesk Associate at InfoTech Solutions. He could feel the resentment and jealousy from some of his coworkers and supervisors as he counted down his last days at the job that was not going to take him anywhere he wanted to go, despite his hard work. He would miss some of his adventures and coworkers there, but the new chapter of his life was leading to greater things including a new job and a future wife.

Most of his belongings were already stored at his parents' house until he moved into his new place. Derek would have no problem finding a roommate around the school to lighten his load. Against the advice of the elder Hooks, Jasper wanted to venture out on his own and start his life with Tina. They begged him to stay there for a few months and save some money, but life with Tina and a better paycheck were too enthralling. He could not be moved for he was a grown man in mind, age, and body despite his naivety.

Tina was in New York fighting with the temptation of the life she knew and staying there for employment. That along with fighting with her parents about her choices was beginning to become unbearable. She longed to be with Jasper again and start living her life with him. She often daydreamed about the ring she would get from him, her wedding (which Mr. Jackson reluctantly agreed to pay for) and how many kids they would have. Her job search was frustrating and painstakingly futile. Even in a large city like Memphis, a person with a degree in finance and no experience would have a hard time finding employment considering the state of the economy. She knew that Jasper had her back even when her parents questioned her. Plus, he was about to embark on a new career with quite a decent salary. She was not really worried at all.

Chapter 6

Stepping into the gigantic front doors of InfoTech Solutions was somewhat overpowering and intimidating. Despite every attempt Jasper made to look like he was cool and calm, his countenance was that of a young, awe-stricken boy on his first trip to Disney World. The culmination of his nervousness, along with a sense of satisfaction and ecstasy peaked as he walked down the small hallway leading to the front lobby. He remembered the first time that he entered these doors. He was a second semester senior on his second job interview ever (the first being his former job at the grocery store). He left a future employee of the company and was now about to begin his first day.

Sheila Bunton, his supervisor, met him at the front reception desk with a warming smile which calmed him somewhat. He then noticed the subconscious turn of the corner of her lips and her eyes looking him up and down a couple of times as he walked closer. He was nervous all over again and wondering if the woman standing in front of him, about 13 years his senior, was going to be reminiscent of that lady boss character on the Eddie Murphy movie, *Boomerang*.

She greeted him, complimented him on his suit, and proceeded to show him around the office. "I am always glad to see talented, young black men from HBCUs come to InfoTech Solutions. I went to Morris Brown myself back in the day. If you care to know, this company is noted for its equal opportunity employment and its Fortune 500 status." As she talked, he thought more about the Eartha Kitt character instead of the Robin Givens character that he had first imaged. Not that she looked old for he thought that she was absolutely stunning, but maybe his mind was playing tricks on him. He swore that she rolled a couple of her R's as she spoke.

She showed him the executive offices on the 12th floor, the various departments throughout the building, the helpdesk area (which he was to be assigned to) and his shift supervisor, Rick, and the human resources area in which he was going to spend most of the morning filling out paperwork. At the end of the tour, he thanked her for the orientation and asked a few questions, trying to sound intelligent and eager as well as showcase the fact that he did his research about the company. He lost count of the number of times Sheila touched his shoulders as they spoke. *Maybe it is innocent, and she is just touchy-feely*, he told himself once. He imagined her going back to her office area once they parted ways and giving a few of her other black female co-workers high fives in her office and bragging about the new, young "whippersnapper" that she has working for her in that Eartha Kitt voice. He subdued his laughter at the thought.

The first day of work for Jasper was exciting and frustrating. He couldn't sleep well the night before and spent a lot of it unpacking and arranging his little apartment. He knew that he was going to feel the agony of fatigue once his nervous energy died down. His shift supervisor kept popping up in the HR department as he was inundated with mounds of forms including everything from insurance forms, emergency contacts, and an entry survey. "Let me know when you are ready, man, and I will show you how we do things around here." Rick seemed very odd to Jasper because he had long silvery hair, a pointy and chiseled chin to accompany his small nose, and black jogging suit with a faded InfoTech Solutions shirt. The company emblem was different from the current one signifying that he had probably been there for a while.

He provided his bank information on a direct deposit form and chose to get paid every two weeks. He listed his parents and Rodney as his emergency contacts on another form. He paused while filling out the beneficiary paperwork and pondered whether he should include his fiancé as a recipient of his benefits if something were to happen to him. He figured since he was going to marry her anyway, and he would do it at some point, he filled out the appropriate section giving her fifty percent and his parents twenty five percent each.

Rick came to grab him shortly before lunchtime and took him to his desk area. He had him fill out more forms like system administrator and nondisclosure agreements. He explained the major helpdesk functions and even how to answer the phone for customers. He broke down in great detail the right and the wrong way to do everything from logging requests to how to do follow-ups. The pride Rick took in his tenure at InfoTech Solutions was evident in his movements and the speech he gave to many other new employees year after year. Some actually moved on to higher positions and other departments, but Rick seemed content with his niche in the company.

Sheila came down to take Jasper to lunch in the on-site cafeteria. The break from Rick was needed, but he wondered if the gesture was one typical to the new employee orientation or that of a personal nature. Either way, a free meal was a free meal in his mind. She was very verbose on the way, randomly jumping subjects, while trying to find out more about him. She actually did roll a few Rs, but it was probably an unnatural, status-induced, bourgeoisie inflection of her voice. He was not exactly turned on by it, but he did slow down a few times to get a few peeks of her curvy shape.

Lunch did end up being like another interview session, but it was more of a personal nature for Sheila "Kitt". The question eventually did come up about his love life, and he almost hesitated as he stated, "I am newly engaged." She didn't really budge off of the subject, but rather dug deeper and inquired more about Tina. Sheila changed the topic after finally saying, "I hope to meet her one day." Jasper thought to himself, *Yeah right, Lady Eloise!*

The rest of the day was typical of a first day: more hand shaking, more forms, meeting coworkers, and time to learn the ropes. At the end of it, Jasper walked to his car and looked at the other cars in the parking lot. Mercedes Benz and BMW logos were everywhere, and Jasper knew that his day was coming to be able to afford one of those. He was happy that his first day went well, and he couldn't wait to tell Tina about it.

Tina was definitely ready to get back to Memphis and her man. She spent about a week and a half at the home of the Jacksons constantly in talks about her future and getting married. She had to endure two interviews that were set up by her mother against her wishes. Tina's time there was intense, with periods where her mother wouldn't even speak to her. It was Mr. Jackson who kept the peace as he reminded his wife of the humble beginnings that they both came from. He was just as concerned, maybe even more, but he trusted the fact that all of the love and support that they showed their little girl, now woman, would guide her steps in endeavors that were going to be new and exciting, painful and rewarding.

One day, he had to harshly get his wife to calm down. He walked in on an argument where she was threatening to cut Tina off financially. "…shacking up with that country negro looks bad, Tina! We worked to get the best for you, but your fast ass behind is chasing that Jasper." The venom in her voice was quite poisonous to the future relationship that Tina would have with her mother, and she chose to stay silent during that particular episode. Her mind was made up, and she was going to go to Memphis to be with Jasper and start her new life, whether her mother supported her or not. "You don't listen to what is best for you, and if it doesn't work out, don't call me crying and asking for money."

That was the point that her dad stepped in. "Shut the hell up, Whitney! Show some damn support for your daughter. Your parents didn't want us together, and I didn't have a job when we started dating. I will hear no more of this rubbish, nonsense!" With that he went to his study, and Tina tearfully went to pack. She ended up leaving a day early to go back to Memphis.

Jasper learned the dos and don'ts quickly at InfoTech Solutions, impressing both Rick and Shelia. In that first week,

Sheila took him to lunch an additional time and dropped a couple of subtle hints of attraction, while she was checking on him and his progress. Mentally twisted, he both wondered if a slight return of attraction would help or hinder his progress at the company. Then again, he was engaged and shouldn't have been thinking like that anyway. His playing days were over, and he knew that the old Jasper would have tried to break Sheila's back in bed and hope that there was very little drama to sift through later.

That Friday, he quickly turned in his time sheet, something that was new to him, and almost ran to his car. Though Tina wasn't due to fly in until 8 p.m. that night, he wanted to ensure that his apartment, their apartment was ready. He vacuumed the place again, and put a dozen roses on the bed in which they would lay. He placed a couple of wine glasses in the freezer and placed a bottle of Pinot Grigio in the refrigerator. The CD meant to set the mood for his act of engagement was postured in the CD player which was set on pause. It was ready to bellow some romantic tune hoping to set the mood once Tina stepped through the door. This was the beginning…the first actual moment of a life together with the woman he loved.

As he prepared to cook the food, the phone rang with a disgruntled Tina on the other end calling before catching her last connecting flight. She stated that her mom called her to give her another chance to change her naïve mind.

Jasper stated, "Don't worry. You are coming home." He felt a surge of energy hit him as the words came out. It seemed like his fiancé didn't even hear him nor returned his excitement.

About an hour later, he sat on his couch rehearsing how he would open the door and what he would say to his beloved as she entered the door. He looked through his music to find an old school CD that he made which had the song "Anticipation" by Con Funk Shun on it. Humming and singing a word here and there, he sat on the couch. He wanted to rest up for an exciting night. He dozed off with affectionate visions and surreal excitement.

Around 9 p.m., he was awakened by Tina knocking on the door, and he jumped up and quickly lit candles and turned on the stove to warm up the food. By the time her knocks became frustrated banging on the door, he opened it with shaking hands and a thumping heartbeat. Tina hugged him and gave him a peck on the lips. She moved past him and said, "Nice place, but we will work on your interior decorating, baby." Jasper was stunned, and his face showed it causing Tina to change her comment. "I mean, it looks good in here, baby. I just had a long day of flying." At that moment, she noticed the flowers, heard the music playing, and smelled the food cooking, which prompted her to run up and kiss the still stunned Jasper. His face loosened, and he went on with his plan as devised.

"Let me give you a quick tour of our little apartment." He was proud of his accomplishment in being able to afford the place near Cordova which was probably smaller than others that rent for the same price, but it was in an up and coming neighborhood. He noticed the look on Tina's face, but stifled a comment when she changed it. The night was going to be special because he had placed such care into it. At the end of the tour, which ended in the bedroom, he grabbed her in a fit of passion. She felt his heart beating frantically and saw the love and nervousness in his eyes. She finally realized that this night was more than a welcome home dinner to Jasper, and she leaned in to kiss him to show her appreciation.

Chapter 7

The mood of the dinner was not as electrifying as Jasper had hoped, but he subconsciously made excuses in his head for Tina; jetlag, fatigue, or that last conversation with her mom. She was really enjoying herself and genuinely happy to be with her man. Talk of the future, the wedding, and interior decorating were some of the topics discussed over wine and a meal prepared with love. Jasper had the type of love that was not only sincere and pure, but it was as if his soul was deeply intertwined with hers. He could feel her moods without spoken words, and notice shifts in her being without seeing.

He felt that something in his fiancé was troubling her and could no longer stay in the illusion of a perfect night. The slow jam CD in the stereo had played in its entirety about three times and was about to begin again with Luther's Vandross's version of "If This World Were Mine" featuring Cheryl Lynn when Jasper bluntly asked, "Ok, what the hell is going on?"

Tina, who was never good at hiding anything, paused and huffed before replying, "Wh...What do you mean?" She knew

Jasper's ability to read her, but wasn't going to say anything that might ruin the atmosphere. She simply smiled and took another sip of wine. She was hoping that he would let it go. A wave of horniness had hit her earlier partially due to what she was sipping and partially due to the love for the man that would do so much for her. She just wanted to feel Jasper inside her and his lips, hands, and muscles on her. She looked up at him with a saucy sensation glowing from her eyes, but quickly diverted it when met with uncut question and confusion beaming from his.

Jasper was the type of person that said what was on his mind, even to his own deficit. It was a trait that he tried to subdue time and time again, but he felt that night was not the night. The spirit of his beloved was stirred and not in a happy, appreciative, loving way. He felt cheated in that he took so much care and love into making that night perfect. It definitely was not what he envisioned. There was no need to hold back, in his mind. His parents always said that communication is the key to any successful relationship, and he wanted to practice that theory right then. He could feel himself about to say, "What is the point to marrying someone that you can't talk to about anything and everything?"

Another Luther song came on breaking the silence between the two lovers. Love was still in the room, but tension was the dominant sensation at that point. "Fuck it, Jasper! What do you want to hear?" He looked at her, but didn't see her. The woman looking back at him was a woman that he couldn't stand. The woman sitting across the faux wooden table smirking looked a lot like the older, meaner, stuck up version of the one he called boo, Ms. Whitney Jackson. Then a tender smile on a beautiful face replaced the menacing scowl that actually made Jasper afraid for a second.

Tina, got up and sat in her lover's lap, who was visibly befuddled with what he thought he just saw. "Baby, I am just worried about getting a job right now. My mom….."

"Wait right there. I told you that I got you covered, baby." Jasper smoothly continued while feeling his nature rise slowly, "It is only a matter of time, boo. Trust me." She smiled and locked her gaze into his as the last words for the next hour were spoken. "Tina, I love you, and together……" It was her turn to cut off his dialogue, but this time with her soft lips.

The rest of the wine became warm overnight sitting next to plates that never made it to the sink. The candles gradually disappeared while Luther and Cheryl got several chances to sing the same song on a CD left on repeat that night. Love, and the act of making love, replaced tension, anger, and any negative emotion that had the potential to have disastrous effects on an event meant to be a storybook start in the next chapter of the lives of Tina and Jasper.

The next morning, Tina rose first before Jasper did his usual 20 minute workout that he did almost every morning. She started to clean up the dishes from dinner the previous night. She wasn't shocked to see that he barely had enough food to make a small breakfast. He always lived like a bachelor with only enough to get by for the moment. Moving on from that plan, she took a deep breath and cooked a decent breakfast for herself while making a list of groceries and personal items.

Jasper woke up to the smell of cooked sausage and smiled. Tina cooked him breakfast after a good night, or so he thought. He walked out of the bedroom to see Tina looking at TV on the couch next to an empty plate and empty frying pans on the stove. He just said "Wow!", and proceeded to do his routine workout of pushups, crunches, squats, etc. in which he looked at himself in the mirror during each rest period.

Tina sat there without moving, just staring at the TV without regard for him and the world around her until Jasper, slightly sweaty, grabbed the plate and tossed it in the sink as a statement saying, "Thanks for my meal." He huffed as he realized that the last pieces of sausage were gone and all of the orange juice was as well. Smiling, Tina walked up behind him and whispered, "You really don't like to keep food around, do ya?"

In response, Jasper looked at her, and said, "You really don't like to say 'Good Morning' before talking shit, do ya?" Jasper smirked and went to the shower. As he passed by the dresser, Tina was on his heels and trying to set off a small sexual episode to start the day. Not really into it, he turned as if to kiss her and closed the bathroom door. She turned the knob to find the door locked.

Kind of shocked, she laid on their bed and noticed a series of printouts, newspapers, brochures, applications, etc. for jobs in the area sitting in the rocking chair by the closet. She looked through them first with the notion that he was sweet for assisting her, but that was replaced quickly with embarrassment and anger, which she would express as soon as the sound of running water stopped.

She stood there fuming about what she was going to say thinking, *What type of hint is he trying to make?* As Jasper turned off the shower, she was about to knock on the locked door when it was opened by him still wet and nude. He bypassed his lover, his boo, to get a fresh towel in his hallway closet with no intent of turning her on though her smile suggested otherwise. He proceeded to move back in the bathroom when Tina blocked his path, suddenly minus her shirt, and said, "What the hell did I do to you? Why you acting like you don't see me here looking all sexy?"

That statement was sort of his last chance in her mind to play it cool with a joke or get immersed in some of her loving before she went off about what was in that chair. Predictably, Jasper continued on past her without even regarding her to dry off and get on with his day. He noticed that one of the newspapers that he got for Tina was now on the dresser and realized what all of the extra was for. He used that as a jab that would open up a can of drama that she was not ready to eat.

"Oh, I see that you found those applications and resume books in the corner. Maybe that can help us keep some more food around, boo." His reference to the food made her think about the fact that she did not make any attempt to cook him breakfast at all, but all she could focus on was the fact that she didn't need his help looking for work. *It will come,* is what she was saying in her mind as fire spewed from her tongue to the one that she just woke up next to, the one she loved, the one that she wanted to spend her life with.

"What the fuck are you trying to say, Jasper? Everybody wasn't as blessed as you to get a job right away. I can't believe that you would fucking play me with your cheap ass. A muthafucka can't even get enough orange juice to swallow a pill around this bitch." She knew that the cursing would take Jasper over the top and dared him with her eyes to say something in response. To her surprise, he laughed as he closed the door. Tina saw the confusing, yet somewhat seductive, smile plastered on his lips then found herself staring at the closed door.

Swimming in Tina's head was the shock of her own words to Jasper as well as the words that her mother berated in her head just days prior. She knew that she was out of line and saw that she only thought about herself that morning. A part of her didn't care that Jasper was mad because she could go home at any time if things didn't work. She could temporarily live off of the money that was placed in a secret account set up by her mom before she flew back to Tennessee.

After a few minutes of cabinets closing, water running, and the toilet flushing, Jasper stepped out of the bathroom still slightly damp and half dressed. He looked at Tina, who seemed lost in thought, on the bed and swiftly ran over to her to give her a kiss on the cheek. As he arose to finish getting dressed, he said without looking at her and stressing certain words, "I know that this is not your standard of living, but umm….this is our place until we together build to make this and ourselves better. You can choose to stay or leave, but that does not change how I feel about you. Umm…..one thing though, don't complain about how I live until you pay some bills around here. I got you until you get on your feet as long as you are making an effort to do what the hell you have to do. Mom and dad don't like what we are doing….whateva. Time to grow up and get off of their stuck up titties....you feel me? Fuck the amount of orange juice in the fridge; you can't even make your man some toast or something." After those words, he walked out of the door leaving an angry, perplexed, and remorseful Tina sitting on the bed amongst job applications and remnants of their passionate night.

Chapter 8

Tina showed some appeasement and penitence by thoroughly cleaning the small apartment and running to the store to purchase more orange juice and food for dinner that night. She thought about her mom a lot and wondered if she was that much like her... nose up in the air, not always appreciative, and never truly satisfied. She vowed to not be her and to make more of an effort to get a job instead.

In the weeks following, there were back and forth bouts of contention between the two lovers as well as moments of intense passion. Jasper continued to go to work and put his all into learning the ropes as Tina made a fairly decent attempt to find employment. Two interviews came and went. Jasper suggested that she shouldn't aim so high with aspirations of booking a major position with a financial firm, etc. Maybe taking an entry level position and earning her way to a more desirable job was feasible, according to Jasper (as he did), but was not really met with agreement.

In the meantime, Jasper would take care of most of the bills and expenses. Tina contributed some, but also did a fair amount of shopping. He took note that his fiancé was spending unnecessary money, but he wrote it off as saved up money or a credit card from her parents. He was positive that things would change and that a job was in her future and saving for their upcoming marriage would continue. Until then, he planned on keeping his bank accounts separate from hers.

At InfoTech Solutions, Jasper's personality and eager-to-learn attitude got him a lateral change in job. It wasn't a promotion for his grade and pay did not change, but he went from being a helpdesk phone operator to helpdesk dispatch support. Basically, his job went from answering requests for IT support, logging trouble tickets, and dispatching other personnel to solve them, to being one of those dispatched. Though his hard work and merit boosted him up, little did he know that a little help from Shelia was going on behind the scenes.

Rick marveled at how well Jasper was doing as well, but was hesitant to make him a dispatch support person. Shelia seldom influenced who should be promoted, whether upwardly or laterally, with no particular pattern of promoting just females black people, etc. Her interest in Jasper seemed a little too coincidental though, and Rick felt that it was on the premise of something else going on. He made it his goal to find out. He remembered how Shelia came to his helpdesk green with inexperience. Now she was telling him who to promote. He wasn't jealous of her success because he loved his position and wouldn't change a thing at all. He just had a slight issue being told what to do by someone with less experience.

One particular day, Jasper noticed a shift in Rick's countenance as he checked his inbox for trouble tickets to be handled that morning. After another night of listening to Tina complaining about money, how small the apartment was, and other subjects he wasn't in the mood for any mess at work. Sadly, work was a sanctuary away from the new domestic life that his dreams and expectations falsely prepared him for.

"Hey there, Mr. Hooks! Good morning to you," Rick gleefully greeted him as usual. After the reply, his voice lowered and deepened, and Jasper could feel Rick move closer behind him as he said, "I noticed that the ladies kinda like ya around here. I heard that Stephanie Hightower placed a ticket in just to get to you to stop by." Something about his laughter after his statement cued Jasper that more inquisitive remarks were coming and that he was up to something.

"She is cute, but it is not like that, man." Jasper looked his supervisor in the eye to sternly show him that he was not up to whatever he was trying to insinuate and to attempt to read his train of thoughts. Rick, undaunted, continued his set up of querying about various ladies in the building trying to hide what he really wanted to know. "Yeah man, we have a lot nice looking chicks around here, Rick but I'm good with what I go home to after work."

He started making his way toward the door after that last statement when Rick said, "Now, I tell you who I wouldn't mind getting a roll in the hay with. That damn, Sheila! If I wasn't married, and she wasn't my boss, I would pin those long legs up. You hear me there, Jap?" Jasper felt the trap that his boss was trying to pull him into. He couldn't be more obvious.

"She alright," Jasper said without even turning around. Then he started his day laughing to himself and thinking how strange Rick was. *What was all that about?*

In the days that followed, it was as if Sheila knew that her name was brought up. Her attention toward Jasper increased considerably and aggressively, yet covertly. No one was suspicious of her attraction towards him other than Rick, so it seemed. Jasper knew what the deal was, but played stupid until Shelia started to get bold with it. He actually considered succumbing to the furtive flirtation, but he knew all too well the possibilities of a woman's scorn once she was hit with unrequited feelings or misunderstood her position after a few lustful nights with no potential of a deeper relationship. The fact that Shelia was the head of the division that he worked in was enough to keep the sin out of his mind. That and the fact that the he was to be married soon also helped to keep his hormones at bay.

One particular day, her subtle hints weren't so subtle before a meeting she held weekly to get updates from her staff, including Rick and sometimes Jasper. Jasper finished up a trouble ticket early and did not want to go back to his desk with the meeting about to begin soon. He stepped into the conference room ten minutes early and found his senior supervisor setting up the projector to show that week's presentation. Before he could exit without being detected, he found himself pinned up against the door.

"I shouldn't be so forward, but there is something about you that is….so attractive. I like the way that you carry yourself, Mr. Hooks." Sheila looked so sincere in how she looked at Jasper. He was usually cool, but the forcefulness exhibited by her was actually exciting him. She continued, "I know that we could never be, but if the thought ever enters your mind, let me know." Jasper gulped as she seemed like she was about to move in for a kiss, but she turned away as if nothing happened. She winked at him and continued setting up for the meeting.

Stunned, Jasper stepped outside to collect his thoughts and sip some water at the nearest fountain. With the way Tina had been acting at home, the invitation seemed quite inviting. Two months had passed, and she was still unemployed and hardly trying to change that status. The excitement of being forever in matrimony seemed distant to how it used to be. The arguments increased while the passionate nights of spontaneity decreased. He felt weird lying to his fiancé about how much money he was bringing in, but it seemed like that was all she cared about. The lover that he could once talk to about anything was fixated on a reality not his own. Shelia represented the drive, ambition, and objectives that he dreamed his darling would encompass. He took a deep breath and entered the conference room again. He was relieved to see Rick and two other people there awaiting the beginning of the meeting. He took his seat and quietly wrote in his notepad.

Rick looked at his young protégé and gave him a quick smirk then looked at his young division chief unbeknownst to either of them. It was nothing personal to "Jap", as he called him, but getting one up on his chief may be beneficial sometime in the future. He was considered one of the old guys of the company. The original InfoTech Solutions employees from his time were being replaced by younger, not necessarily brighter, men and women who lacked the common sense and work ethic of his generation. He had seen his share of those coming and going, and the thought of being next on the chopping block or a casualty of salary caps occasionally crept into his mind. Jap was a good guy, but job security was more important.

Eventually, the meeting started, and Shelia received the reports from all of her subordinate leaders or their representatives. Jasper could feel Rick's eyes on him off and on during the meeting. *What the hell was he thinking about? Maybe Shelia was too obvious? Did he know something? Maybe he wished that Shelia was flirting with him?* He played it off as if he didn't notice Rick looking or Shelia wanting. No pussy that he was not getting was going to ruin all that he worked for.

At the end of the meeting, Shelia discussed items such as evaluations, budget cuts, and some other notes. She was concluding when she stated, "It's almost time for the Annual ProtectCon Security Conference in Virginia. Usually someone from each department in our division goes, but the CEO is only authorizing a few compared to last year. Submit a couple of names by next week's meeting, and I will pass those names on. Other than that, thanks and have a good day people."

Jasper had never heard of ProtectCon, but saw his supervisor and a few others perk up. He wondered what all of the fuss was about.

DeMarcus Hunter was awarded a fellowship to pursue his Masters degree and assist a couple of professors. Summer school and his fellowship had already started. Though most students went home during the summer, the partying did not stop for those who remained. Every weekend, someone was having a barbeque, pool party, or something at their house or apartment. At several of these get-togethers, DeMarcus ran into Tara.

Tara was in summer school to take a couple of classes that she had dropped previously. It was just a typical summer for her as a student full of classwork, a part-time job, and hanging out as much as possible. She caught DeMarcus looking, possibly staring, at her at some of the parties she was able to go to. He even showed up at her job a couple times to buy a few items. She thought nothing of it until he boldly approached her after having a few drinks at a Pembrook football player's house.

"Hey there sexy. Looking good tonight....too good to be sitting here by yourself."

"What? What did you just say?" Tara was wondering if he was just being nice or trying to make a move. It was obvious that the liquor in his system had either increased his courage or lessened his nervousness.

Fearless, DeMarcus looked at Tara with a kind of hunger and yearning. "Excuse me if my compliment bothered you, baby, but I just wanted to let you know that you were looking good. You already knew that though." He laughed a little as he waited for a response. He assumed what she was going to say next.

"Umm….you know that I used to date your frat brother? Did he put you up to this shit? Because I ain't got time for this shit."

As she kept talking, DeMarcus jumped in to cut her off, "Whoa! Can't a playa just give a sexy woman a compliment? I know about you and Jasper, but he all engaged now to that Tina chick." That piece of knowledge felt like a blow to her stomach. She felt that they would never be together again, but marriage seemed so final. She seemed removed from reality, lost in what was just told to her and tuned out to whatever he was saying.

DeMarcus noticed the shocked look on her face and decided to use it to his advantage. He continued the flirtatious wordplay, and as Tara recovered from her thoughts she heard, "So, I say never mind Jasper. You can't be unhappy while he is living with someone else. You know what I'm saying?"

Trying to hold back a tear, she took a deep breath and said, "What are you saying again, DeMarcus?"

He realized that he had her by the look in her eyes. She was still in shock, but he felt that his homeboy walked away from one of the finest women Pembrook ever had to walk on the campus. He wanted her even before Jasper had her. *He fucked up on this one, and I want to tackle that and get at that soft-looking ass a few times.* His thoughts translated into saying to her, "Look Tara. I am just saying that you seem like you are cool to hang out with. There ain't shit to do in Pembrook, so hit me up sometime when you get bored." She walked away with his number, and he walked away to get another drink and plan on how he would achieve his goal. *Fuck Jasper.*

Chapter 9

Weeks later, Tina and Jasper went to a snow cone spot near Whitehaven High School to cool off from the summer heat and attempt to cool down their emotions after another night of disagreements, making up, and more disagreements. Tina came to that particular location often to get a small cup of shaved ice at least twice a week; each time the same flavor. That Saturday was no different other than the fact that Jasper accompanied her.

There was no magic between Tina and Jasper in the week leading up to the Saturday outing. The couch became a second bedroom some nights for Jasper, constantly and perhaps subconsciously. At this time, marriage talk wasn't as frequent or exciting for either of them. Jasper did not want to see all the time and feelings that he invested into the relationship fall to nothing, but the life he was living was not ideal for him. There was so much more he wanted; he wanted what his mom and dad had.

Tina was touched by a moment of sadness that morning and invited Jasper to come with her for her Saturday routine. As she stated, "It will be my treat." Jasper unknowingly sneered. She had to do something to make Jasper fall in love with her again or she felt that she would be homeless soon. Her parents barely answered her phone calls anymore, or made statements like, "No job yet, huh?" or "How much do you need?" The money placed in a special account for her was starting to dry up. There was no more money for good grades or just being daddy's little girl. She was grown now, and they reminded her of it constantly.

Jasper visibly was mentally worn out and his heart was frayed by the lack of ambition that Tina exhibited. It was more than money for he made enough to pay the bills. It was the lack of forward thinking that his woman had. If she wasn't that concerned about getting her priorities in order now, how would she do as a mother someday or if Jasper ever got hurt? Every attempt to convey this to her was met with excuses of economic issues and just wanting to relax a while after college, among others reasons.

Daddy Hooks use to always do a little exercise with his son that seemed so relevant now. He would have Jasper put his arm straight out in front of him with his hand folded inward blocking his vision past it asking him to stare at it as he talked. At some point, he would ask him to drop his hand, while keeping his arm straight and ask him what he sees. Then he would ask him to put his hand back up and continue to talk to him as he stared at his hand. The second time that he asked him to drop his hand, he sometimes would have some type of treat for him. He would explain the exercise as such, "Listen son, as you stay focused on only what is right in front of you, you can't always see what else is around you, what your future could have in store for you and what dangers could come at you. When you drop your hand, you can still see what's in your field of view, but you can also see what is around you as well. Basically son, I am saying that see the hand as a goal that you are trying to reach among others around you. If you stay focused on just that goal, you may blind yourself to what is around you, unable to see anything else." Right now, Jasper saw that Tina's hand was figuratively in front of her face and not moving.

They didn't speak much since Jasper was trying to not bring up the same subjects, and Tina was trying to not to bring up a subject that may lead to another verbal quarrel. He wanted to tell her about the continuous drama at work, but didn't want to talk about or be accused of cheating with Shelia. They sat in silence eating the frozen indulgence full of flavored syrup. Tina finally said that a friend offered to help her out and try to get her a position in human resources somewhere. Jasper looked at her as if to say, *I've heard you say stuff like that before*.

Tina continued to plead somewhat for a little more faith in her as she apologized several times for acting like her mom and not being a grown-up. She choked up as she said, "Baby, I miss the excitement that we had. I want to make you a proud wife one day, and I ain't doing a good job so far, huh?"

"Well boo, you can change that starting now." Smiling with lips slightly stained a bright blue color from his shaved ice he accepted her apology and promised that he would give her more time and support in her job search. "I am glad that we had this talk, but I gotta go meet Rodney at Jo Jo's." After a long embrace they parted ways, both with optimism and Tina thankful that she wasn't homeless yet.

Jasper returned to his car and saw a missed call from Kyle. Kyle was beginning his second phase of the Officer Basic Course for his appointed specialty in the Army. He was about to go to lunch and study with some of his classmates when his old friend called him back.

"Jasper, what's good with ya? You on your way to see Rodney and his band?"

"Yeah, I was just talking to Tina and eating some shaved ice." He knew the conversation would shift immediately as he said his fiancé's name. "I am on my way to Jo Jo's now."

Jo Jo's Bar and Grill was a popular club near Beale Street that hosted different events from time to time. Memphis was always known for its musical roots and Jo Jo's has been around for years adding musical relevance to the area. Rodney and his band were in their third week of their gig when he extended an invitation to several of his friends and former classmates. Jasper canceled all plans to be there later that evening, even if Tina wasn't going to join him.

Through the phone, Jasper felt the question coming up his buddy's throat after a pause. "So ummm….ummm, Tina working yet?"   Before Jasper could reply, Kyle all knowingly continued with, "What's up with her? It's like she is jealous of your success and shows it by not getting her own?" He continued for a few more minutes, not waiting for any reply or rebuttal. By the time Jasper was able to get in a word, he was almost at his destination. He knew that the more he talked, the more debate would occur. Considering that, he stayed quiet that time until he walked up to the club.

"Hey mane, I am at the place. I ain't got time to talk about that mess right now. You feel me? She is working on some things, and it will be aight in the end. Cool?" He knew that his homeboy was just looking out for him, but he also saw what was seen by others. He told Tina that he would give her some time, and he was going to hold to his word….at least for a while longer.

Kyle had to get back to studying and not wanting to talk to his former roommate about what seemed so obvious and chose to let it go. "Aight pimp. I'll holla at you later." With that, the two hung up their phones and Jasper strolled up into Jo Jo's.

The ambiance in Jo Jo's was magical and awe-inspiring. The pictures on the walls were of historic achievements and troubles, legends and newcomers. The place made one feel laid back and excited at the same time. The feelings evoked by the place were stirred by something more than material décor, by something deeper than the rich colors painted on the walls, by something louder than the horns that played week to week. The spirits of the forefathers of blues and soul seemed to be present, and they were telling their stories without music or words. It wasn't Jasper's first time going there, but seeing his friend and the band setting up seemed to be dream-like compared to the other times he had been there. Later, he saw his talented friend sitting at a table with a few other people.

Though Rodney was not the leader of the band called Dipped in Soul, he was giving some instruction to his band mates on a song that they were going to try out that evening. Talking and playing music was like breathing to Rodney; he needed it. This need was quite apparent in his face and evident in his hand movements. The others listened intently and shared his enthusiasm as they tuned instruments or took notes. He suddenly turned to see Jasper standing behind him and listening with just as much enthusiasm, along with some pride.

"Oh snap! Everyone, this is my homeboy Jasper. He was there when I used to practice in the dorms, and I used to keep him up all night when I was trying to figure a song out."

Jasper replied jokingly with, "And you still suck." He was then introduced to the other band members who consisted of one guitar player/lead singer, a female singer, two keyboard players, and a drummer. Rodney played the bass guitar and sometimes sang lead as well. Jasper had to avoid eye contact with the sexy, caramel colored female singer because just how she moved her lips rose his temperature. With the issues that he had been having with his fiancé, he found himself losing control of suppressing his attraction to other women. Sonya noticed his uneasiness and made a mental note to ask Rodney about his slim, attractive friend.

Twenty minutes of casual conversation, drinks, and last minute instructions eased the nervousness before their final practice before the show later. The lead singer barely did any conversing and reminded Jasper of one of those guys that tried too hard to look smooth. He looked like the type that would do two hundred pushups, put a leather jacket on his bare, baby-oiled chest and lick his lips a little too much like L.L. Cool J used to do, just to impress a woman at a club. One would think that Rodney was the leader of the group. His natural ability to decipher notes and scales was astonishing as well as his ability to lead, and older or younger, all the other members were receiving an education.

As the practice began, Jasper checked his phone to see if Tina had returned any of his text messages that he sent earlier. Not yet. He looked up at the stage and saw Sonya glancing at him between songs. The urge to make whatever she was visualizing come true was strong, but he knew that his will to do right by Tina was even stronger. He focused his attention on how his comrade was playing his instrument like it was a part of him. Curtis Sampson, also known as Jo Jo, sat by Jasper watching his friend and said, "That bass player is playing that thang like he…..he sold his soul to the damn Devil himself and fought him to get it back. Damn." Jasper knew that the escape that music gave him probably kept his friend sane considering all that he has gone through in his past. He validated what blues really meant and defined it just like many before him that played at Jo Jo's, on Beale Street, and in Memphis.

Hours later, Jasper traveled to his little apartment in Cordova. It was between sets of Dipped in Soul that he made his exit. He enjoyed the time that he spent with Rodney, and talking to him is what he felt he needed to truly give the pending marriage a fair shot. Tina did finally return the texts sent to her and stated that she was asleep. Knowing how much she napped, it was no question in his mind.

He pulled up to his place a little after 8 p.m. with a box of condoms and some take-out from Jo Jo's. He wanted to certify his revelation with some steamy, intense sex to nullify the tension between them. He had renewed faith that all would be fine for him and his future. Something about the music he heard earlier invigorated him and renewed his spirit. He already had a few words planned, but he aimed to communicate with his body more so than his words.

As he walked inside, it seemed like Tina had read his mind. Jasper was the type of guy that was more turned on by a nude woman walking toward him versus wearing lingerie, but she was sitting on the couch in a new two-piece outfit colored a shimmering peach hue. No need for conversation for the message was clear; she belonged to him and desired to drown their divergence from what they used to be in a mind-blowing encounter meant to erase all doubt and forever solidify their future together.

Unspoken sessions like that for them were not uncommon. A look would turn into a smile, a smile would turn into a kiss, a kiss would turn into two lovers breathing hard after affection fluids and sweat soaked the sheets in a passion-scented room. Instantaneously, the soon-to-be married couple ravished each other hungrily. Groping and giggling, touching and teasing began that night's session without any apology to any neighbors that might catch an errant moan or two.

Jasper later went to bed feeling satisfied in more than one way. He watched Tina sleep only wearing her top when a text message buzzed his phone. Rodney's text said, *Thanks for coming out bruh! Tonight was awesome. I hope that shit with you and Tina works out. If not, Sonya told me to tell you hello. LOL.* Jasper chuckled as he read that last part. Then he set his alarm clock before snuggling next to his woman.

Weeks later, all seemed well with the two lovers. Tina had a couple of interviews and was waiting for one particular company to call her back. Everything between them wasn't perfect, but communication and compromises got better with time which is to be expected from two people as they learn to live together. Money was still tight, but the two seemed to be making it just fine without any assistance from their parents. Jasper stayed true to his belief on not sharing bank accounts until Tina got a job.

Chapter 10

People usually leave their homes on the way to work, school, etc. with expectations on how the day will go, whether good or bad. One particular morning, Jasper woke up wondering if Shelia would make another move to seduce him, or if a customer would approach him arrogantly asking for help while trying to explain their opinionated answer. He was expecting it to be a typical day for him.

Jasper had worked out before he showered and got dressed before leaving the apartment. He had to fight off Tina's advances to ensure that he would not be late to InfoTech. He checked a couple of emails and grabbed some fruit on the way out the door. He left Tina lying in bed talking to her mom. Weeks later, she was still unemployed. She was dipping into some reserve money that she had been saving over the years from her affluent parents. Jasper thought that it was wise of her to do that over the years since most young people with well-to-do parents usually spent all that was given, then asked for more. He, on the other hand, only broke that glass in case of an emergency. He came from a long line of hustlers who worked for what they needed and wanted.....always.

Walking to the car, he waved to a couple of the children walking to the school bus stop. He wolfed down an apple and started on his banana in the car before pulling off. He listened to his favorite Eightball and MJG CD for a couple of songs to get motivated for the day ahead. Lately, he had noticed that Rick was acting even stranger than normal; so strange that he had to mention it to Shelia. She dismissed it as, "Oh, that is just how he is." Playing music in his car before he drove to work was becoming a ritual for him. After listening to his favorite song "Pimps", he started his car and rolled out of the apartment complex.

Twenty minutes later, he parked in the massive parking lot of InfoTech Solutions and grabbed his things. As he locked the door, he realized that he left his identification badge at home. Cursing quite audibly, he jumped in his car to call Rick, which he did not want to do. His attendance record had been perfect up until that point. A few attempts later, he had not reached Rick or anyone else in the office to let them know. Sucking his teeth, he decided to make another phone call that he really didn't want to make.

Shelia answered on the first ring, and said "Hey there, superstar. Excuse me….how can I help you, Mr. Hooks?"

"Ma'am, I um…left my badge at home. I made it all the way to the building and saw that I left it. I wanted to let someone know before I went back home to get it. I tried to call Rick, but ummm…."

"It's ok. I will let him know. You can just work the time on the back end of the day or something. Go ahead and hurry back." She said that last part in her characteristic flirtatious way and rolling of the R's. Jasper rolled his eyes and said, "Ok." He hung up and started the trek home. Traffic was definitely going to be heavier with many others trying to get to their respective jobs, schools, or wherever their destinations were.

He futilely sped through traffic trying to save as much time as possible, but he had a gut feeling that he would not be back at InfoTech until late morning. He lifted his phone to call Rick again, in case Shelia didn't tell him, but placed the phone down back on his passenger seat. He turned up his stereo playing "Armed Robbery" by Eightball and MJG as if the rapid progression of the beats would make him go faster. All he could think about was the fact that he was still in his first six months of employment and was about to be late.

About forty minutes later, he hastily and crookedly parked his car trying to save every second that he would have to make up some time that week. He didn't even lock the doors since he was going to rush in, grab his badge (maybe some more fruit), and run back to be on his way. He was thinking that Tina was probably still laying around in her PJs as he noticed that her car didn't move from the same spot that it was in that morning. He made a note to discuss that point if they were to ever get in the job search conversation again.

He opened the door and instantly went for his badge on the kitchen counter. He was full of adrenaline from his rushed drive back to the apartment. Before he called his woman's name, he thought he heard some voices in his bedroom. The adrenaline eased a little bit as he hesitated, but it spiked up all of a sudden as he actually listened to what he was hearing.

There comes a moment of disbelief and doubt when something unbelievable happens to you that you heard stories about or only saw in movies. One may lose focus of what is transpiring and stop to question how real the moment is. Jasper was trapped, dragged into that moment just then. He thought he actually heard Tina moaning softly, but couldn't hear it clearly as his own heartbeat seemed to drown it out. The moan didn't sound like the way she moaned when they made love. He wondered why he would think about that at such a time and frowned in response. He stood frozen in place, his ears ringing with his own voice questioning what was happening. He wasn't even sure if he was thinking the questions or if he was actually saying them out loud.

Before he knew it, he was at the door of his own bedroom, which was never usually closed.

A multitude of feelings were battling inside of his head as he was straining to make sense of reality and his imagination. Thump, thump; his heart was racing as he was trying to tell himself that he thought that Tina had a vibrator and was making use of it early that morning. Thump, thump; she wasn't the type to use vibrators. Thump, thump; the bed was slightly squeaking and a rush of rage pumped inside him as his eyes widened and he unknowingly held his breath. The door was slightly opened so he stealthily positioned himself by the door praying that he was wrong about what was so apparent. Thump, thump; he almost fainted as a deep voice shouted, "Damn Tina, shit!"

There was no denying it at that point, and it was verified as he widened the slim angle of the door just enough to see the mirror on his dresser. A tear of perhaps sadness or anger cooled a sliver of his burning face as he saw his fiancé, his boo, lying over a pillow on the bed, their bed. From the position he was in, he could only see a set of dark hands grasping her derriere the way he used to and thrusting fondly. Tina didn't look as if she was enjoying the act, but it was still happening. She was letting it happen.

He fell backwards with his hands shaking so bad that he could not stand up or shut the door back. He had to see who was doing this to Tina, to him. Each effort to stand up was difficult and failed. Another tear dropped down the other cheek as all noise seemed to cease leaving him alone in a void unable to hear, feel or move. Then he heard, "Oh girl, this ass…is…so sweet, so sweet, shit!" The fire in his body flared like putting lighter fluid on a lit grill. He found the ability to move again toward the door. He crawled back to the door, purely motivated by wrath, and looked in the mirror. He couldn't believe that no one heard a sound. Through tear covered eyes, he looked into the closed eyes of the offender of his place and lady in the mirror. He looked at his own frat brother, Tim Conley, vigorously humping away with no finesse. He looked back at Tina in the mirror, who was just unemotionally lying there letting it happen.

He fought the urge to just run in the door and smack Tim in the back of the head and punch Tina in the middle of her naked back. He fought back the tears even harder. If the episode was over in his bedroom, the two cheaters would have seen Jasper hysterically gasping for air and shaking his head. His hands couldn't stay still, alternating between fists and shaking fingers. It took him a moment to gather his thoughts, but a slight gasp from Tina woke him up from his private pandemonium. He had to get out of there or he felt that jail time was in his very near future.

Almost as quietly as he walked in, he strolled toward the front door and looked back at his little apartment. It may have not been much, but he saw it was the first home that he wanted to share with the one he would never call boo again. He opened the door, wiped another tear from his cheek and then proceeded to make a beeline to his car. He forgot about Rick, Shelia, InfoTech, and his future marriage…everything. Only getting out of there before he killed someone was the goal.

He reached the car and fumbled with his keys as his hands continued their frenzied fidgeting. He had to stop and take a deep breath before he continued. Finally, he opened his door and sat in silence with only the muffled sounds of the neighborhood keeping him company. He went to start the car and just happened to look at Tina's car. "Whoa!" is the only thing he could say when he recognized the car parked next to Tina's was Tim's car. He cringed as he looked at the metallic car tag on it innocently showing the fraternity letters that Jasper proudly displayed every chance he got.

Without any further hesitation, he hopped out of his vehicle with a purpose. The animal in him was loose when he ran up the stairs skipping a couple here and there. He then stopped at the top of the stairs and smiled. An epiphany halted his movement, and a plan of sickening absurdity flashed in his mind. He had left the front door unlocked, but that didn't matter. He, a little too calmly, wiped the last teardrop that he would shed and reached for the phone in his pocket.

His supervisor actually picked up on the first ring that time. "Sir, I was rushing home to find my badge and I almost got hit by a truck trying to get here so fast. Do you mind if I make up the hours for today up over the rest of the days in this pay period?" The lie was simple, but Rick could hear the sincerity of something terribly wrong in his voice.

"Sure Jap. Shelia told me that you left your badge. Hell, it happens to us all from time to time. Are you ok? Is everything ok there, guy?" Despite the feelings he had against his own supervisor, Rick prided himself in being personable and approachable by his subordinates. Jasper confirmed that he was ok, and Rick ended the conversation with, "Ok, we'll see you tomorrow."

Smiling again at both the fact that his lie passed and what he was about to do, he positioned himself on the wall by the door. He pretended to be on the phone to avert suspicious neighbors and waited. He hoped what was going on inside would end soon for he was so ready to compensate for his hurt feelings.

As Tim walked out the door twenty minutes later, he was met with a punch to his left cheek from Jasper. Shocked, he screamed, "Oh shit!" similar to the way he did while he was standing over Tina. Before he could rise and recover, he was met with three more emotional and swift punches to the head and chest. Seeing the fourth punch coming his way, he realized that he was not being robbed. He realized that he got caught by one of his fraternity brothers that always had his back. A mix of fear, shame, and sadness punched him in the gut before that punch landed.

Tina was washing up in the bathroom when she heard the ruckus. She also was suspecting that Tim was being robbed in broad daylight so she ran toward the door. As she threw the shirt over her head, she noticed Jasper's badge in the middle of the floor only feet away from the bedroom door. *Caught* was the only thought that she had and retreated back to the bathroom, terrified.

After the session of pummeling, Jasper still did not feel satisfied. Tim was lying on his side breathing heavily, his hand over his right eye. Despite his size, he was no match for the element of surprise and the fueling hatred from betrayal. His acceptance of his wrong doing was just to lay there. Without being prompted, he turned to see Jasper standing over him shaking his head with a look of such disdain that he almost turned back around. "Man, I am sorry….so sorry frat. She called me and said that it was cool."

"What?!?" Jasper felt his legs go weak so he didn't have the energy to kick the downed chump. "What the hell you just say?"

"Man, I will tell you everything. Just let me get up." He was still breathing hard….and don't hem me up man….please."

Just hearing him beg to not get hit almost sparked Jasper to do it again. *How dare he come up in my place, do what he did, and then ask to not get his ass kicked?* Tim begged again, "Please!"

As he stumbled and leaned against the wall, Tim wondered why Tina did not come out at all. She approached him about getting some sex from time to time for a cost. He felt stupid for even paying for sex, especially getting caught for paying for sex. Jasper in his tremulous mind still didn't grasp what was going on. Afraid of getting hit again, Tim just confessed since he could tell that his fraternity brother was too angry and confused.

"Listen, man. I am so sorry. She would call me up to give her $200 to fuck her every blue moon." Jasper flinched when the word fuck was said. "Man, she said she needed the money because she couldn't find a job. My bad brother, I feel bad." That is when Jasper swung with a force full of love for his cheating fiancé and the betrayal of two people that he cared about. The punch didn't knock Tim out, but he wasn't going to move for a while after that.

In the bathroom, Tina sincerely prayed for her life. The scuffle that she heard outside was destined to be worse for her. She was mad at herself for leaving her cell phone in the bedroom and unable to call for help. Regardless, she was not going to open that door. That door was the only barrier to keep her from looking in the eyes of the man that she loved and hurt at the same time. That door was the only barrier to keeping the shame and dirtiness that she was feeling contained. That door was the only barrier possibly saving her life.

She heard some shouting every now and then, but couldn't make out any words. She replayed how it all started, how that moment came to be. *If only my parents kept giving me money instead of cutting me off. This damn economy made it too hard to find a job. I had to do something. Jasper kept pressing me to get a damn job.* Her thoughts were interrupted when the door that she swore she had locked suddenly opened.

Jasper threw the hanger that he had used to pick the lock inside the tub before entering. Tina, still half-dressed, sat on the commode shaking. He didn't enter the bathroom right away. He just stood there shaking his head and smiling. The smile was reminiscent of the moment when characters in movies become the bad guy. Evil and misery were visible in his expression, and this made Tina cry out in fear.

"Baby, baby....I....I can explain!" Jasper stood there almost about to cry himself, but he promised that he had cried his last tear. He stood there because he knew that if he touched her violence would occur. "Jasper baby......I was running out of money and....please baby.....let's talk about it....I....it's just.....please...." She mumbled like that for a few minutes. The man that kissed her on the cheek before he left hours ago was standing there clenching his fists and not saying a word.

"Stop! Let me get this straight!" Jasper stopped her confusing talk with a firm statement showing that her time to explain was over.

"So you were sleeping with my fucking frat brother, of all people, for fucking money? How many other muthafuckas you been fucking? Up in our....my crib? How long have you been doing this shit? Fuck it. I don't want to know. Was he the only one? I really don't want to know that." Jasper paused for a while to collect his thoughts and hide the crackle in his voice that was about to come.

Tina almost said something, but his look back at her was definitely saying, *Shut up bitch!* She retreated any effort to apologize anymore. She thought that she would have never gotten caught. Jasper was predictable, she needed money, and Tim was known to pay a lot of cash just to sniff a woman. She knew that it was over before Jasper's next words came out. She wondered where she would go for home was not an option. Her mind was churning about what to do next as her man just stared, smiled, and shook his head. Jasper didn't get mad often, but those were the times that he was unpredictable.

"Is Tim ok?" Those were the words that slipped out of Tina's mouth and through the tense silence in that bathroom. If it was even possible for Jasper's face to tighten up anymore, it did as those words came out. That was a big mistake.

"Huh…did you…what….oh hell naw!" Any thoughts of keeping Tina around fleeted like a group of birds being shot at. Jasper, unbeknownst to him, dropped another tear as he spoke. "Tina, I am about to go to work. When I get back, you and your shit better be gone. No notes, flowers, no shit to say sorry or give you another chance. Don't cook, make up the bed, or leave a fucking earring." Tina actually thought that she saw Jasper's whole body wobble. "Remember….baby….you did this….you….did this."

With those final words, Jasper walked back to pick up his badge on the floor and left the apartment. He didn't turn back to look at the one he used to call boo, kiss on the forehead and make love to constantly. He simply walked out slowly somewhat daring her to say something, run up behind him, or even move. He closed the door and he was gone out of his place and out of Tina's life.

Tina could only sit there and cry loudly when the door latched shut.

Chapter 11

In the days that followed, Jasper dug into his job to ease his mind from random thoughts of loneliness, anger, and pain. He worked as much overtime that was allowed claiming that he was saving up for a new car. Rick appreciated the enthusiasm displayed in his star worker, but it was clear that something was different. Shelia noticed too.

Rodney and Kyle made several attempts to break the steel wall of emotion displayed by their homeboy. They had several phone conversations about how to get Jasper out of his slump. They talked about taking actions like cursing Tina out, hooking him up with some people they knew, or even calling Tara. One particular evening they teamed up for a three way phone call conversation, but the futile effort to console their buddy only ended in argument. The two roommates decided to let their friend get over it on his own, but promised to jump back in if he started getting too depressed or irrational.

Then there was Tina. She called a few times begging for forgiveness and a second chance. All phone calls went unanswered and all text messages were instantly deleted. Unbeknownst to Jasper, she had stayed with Tim for a couple days until she moved back to Pembrook to stay with one of her sorority sisters. She kept up the charade to her parents that she and Jasper were just fine and that more interviews were coming.

Through rumor, Ms. Jackson learned about her daughter's exodus to the city of her school. Curious to gather some truth in order to squelch the rumors among her circle, she phoned her daughter. Of course, Tina dodged the questions and attempted to change the subject. "Listen Tina, I already know the damn truth. Did that boy do something to you? I told you not to shack up with that country bumpkin…"

She went on and on until Tina couldn't take being chastised anymore. Not taking full responsibility for her acts, she mouthed off, "Well, since you and Dad cut me off from any money, I had to do what I had to do. You could have kept me up a lil longer. Y'all got the money, and I have been trying to get a job! I really have been trying."

"What!?!" Confused, Ms. Jackson pushed for more information and was told about not finding the right job, but she stated that she didn't have money to do her share staying at Jasper's place. Without money, she was becoming desperate. That is when Tim came into the picture joking about how much he would pay to get a piece of her one day at one of the local malls. For an hour, Tina explained in detail the events that got her to the point she was at. She constantly talked about Jasper with phrases like, "I just love him so much", "I wish that I could take it back", and "If it wasn't for this doggone economy".

She felt like she had no other choice. Tina's mom was shocked by her beyond moralistic actions, but felt somewhat responsible for her daughter going through all of that. She felt compelled to offer some financial assistance and promised not to tell her dad. She calmed her daughter down and told a story of her own as well.

"Baby, I had to do some strange things to get your father to take me seriously. See, I knew that he was going to be something when we were in dental school together. You could just tell. There was another female student that had caught his eye, but I wasn't going to let her take my man." Tina attentively sat there astonished with the revelation coming from her mother just then. She continued, "That bitch thought that she was so cute and so smart! I acted like I needed some additional tutoring during a particular phase, and I targeted your father. He was one of the top of the class and was happy to help a sista out. Just as he was getting comfortable assisting me, I moved in and made sure that he would never forget me."

Tina, still in shock, was trying not to imagine the seductive and deceptive acts her mother probably committed, but she got the gist of what her mother was saying. Ms. Jackson said then what she meant. "Sometimes, Tina, you have to do what you gotta do….if you want your man." She didn't really like Jasper, but something in her did not like to see her daughter hurting like she was. There was no way in her mind that a country boy was going to do this mess to her daughter because he was not worthy of such a refined woman.

The experience was oddly a bonding moment between a mother and daughter whose estranged relationship and tense filled interactions were probably due to generational differences but more attributed to how similar their personalities were. They recognized it during that conversation more than ever. Tina was devising a complex and wily plan to get her man back, and its inception was going to be something that Jasper would never forget.

The conflict between Tina her mother may have been easing, but things seemed to be getting uneasy around InfoTech Solutions. Rick's suspicions about his subordinate and his superior had become grossly apparent to Jasper, Shelia, and others in their division. Shelia and Jasper ignored the accusations and rumors even though Shelia wished there was some truth to them. Though Jasper ignored them, it was becoming more and more annoying coming to work, especially after having his heart broken. He just was not his usual cheerful self, considering the mess swirling around him.

One light in his barrel of darkness was that he was selected to go to ProtectCon to represent the company. He found out at one of the weekly divisional meetings. Shelia explained that her boss had a hand in the matter and personally chose Jasper and two other employees. She also announced that she was going to attend as well to give a presentation. Jasper and Shelia both were subconsciously avoiding eye contact from Rick who was definitely suspicious, blatantly suspicious. Jasper was excited to get away from Memphis for a few days since being in the apartment alone sometimes brought pangs of sadness.

After the meeting, Rick was not shy about his disappointment in not going, but he congratulated Jasper on his selection nonetheless. "So Jap, you gonna finally get a chance to be alone and get a piece of ol' Shelia, huh? That callipygian figure could use a young stud like you, huh?" Jasper looked at his supervisor with sheer anger. He wasn't sure if he was angrier about how Rick kept insisting that something sexual was amidst between Shelia and him or how Rick said "callipygian" as if he didn't know what it meant. He knew what it meant. "Your girl wouldn't know a thing, man!"

There are times when a person has to stand up to an opposing force even if it means future detriment. Sometimes winning the little battles makes the war a lot easier down the line, win or lose. Jasper Hooks was a flurry of frustration at that moment and common sense and respect were fleeting. He was tired of being hurt, tired of being angry, and tired of dealing with his hippie boss who seemed to be more interested in his personal life than his professional development. He felt himself starting to snap.

"Rick, please….not today, sir. It has been a rough time for me lately. I can't sleep, I am backed up on work orders, and my girl slept with my frat brother. The last thing I need is my boss joking about me sleeping with his boss!" He blinked after realizing what he just said, but he was glad that it came out. The jokes had gotten old. He didn't want the extra attention. *I never knew that a hippie could be so mean. I thought that hippies were always happy.* He looked up after a mini staring contest with Rick to see that Shelia was standing ten feet away with her arms crossed. *Oh shit!* Being new to the company he had not accrued a lot of leave time, but he asked to take the rest of the day off. He had taken a few days and hours off already and made up most of them, but he needed to leave just then. He didn't care, and Rick finally realized that Shelia was walking toward them. Voice cracking, he mumbled, "Ok Jap. We will see ya tomorrow."

Angrier with himself for letting Tina affect him like that then his last interaction with Rick, he made his way to the elevator . As the door started to close he overheard Ms. Bunton say to Rick, "Callipygian? Really Rick? Well let's talk about my callipygian figure in my office!" If in a better mood, Jasper would have laughed at the chastising of his superior. All he wanted to do was get to his bed at home, which was a place once filled with passion and adoration....now filled with thoughts of unfaithfulness and foolishness. He remembered that Tina's scent was still on one of the pillows. He told himself that he would sleep with it one last time.

Once he got to the car he checked his voicemails and text messages. He was glad to see that Tina made no attempt to contact him that day. Rodney and Kyle had both send text messages checking on him. He could tell that his homeboys had been talking and were concerned that he was acting extreme. He received a voicemail from his mom stating that she hadn't spoken to him in over a week. That was unusual, and the sound of her voice had that concerned mother's tone to it. *I bet that Kyle and Rodney told her some shit.....or did Tina call trying to get me to talk to her?* He didn't respond to anyone and started to travel to his apartment.

He went to pick up some food at a nearby fast food joint. While in the drive-thru line, the song changed from a recently up-to-date song about the singer's exploits to prove that he is what some woman really needed and wanted to an old Luther Vandross song that he hadn't heard in years. He paused and keyed in on the words, each word further explaining his anguish, his pain, and possibly the truth of his situation. Luther soulfully bellowed Burt

Bacharach's beloved hit, "Anyone Who Had a Heart" through the speakers. The car seemed to inch itself further in the line as Jasper stared lost, more like dazed, through his front windshield. His torn heart was singing in agreement with the man on the radio.

The lady working at the drive thru window attempted to hand Jasper his food about the time in the song the saxophone kicked in strong toward the end. Though her mind was occupied with getting the ever-growing line down so she could take her final break of the day, she seemed to be drawn in a bit by the sadness of a man who was hungry for something more than the high calorie food in the bag. She felt a pinch of what he was feeling as she recognized the song coming out of the broken-hearted man's speakers. She could feel herself about to say "It will be ok, baby." but only "Sir! Your food!!" came out instead.

She caught a glimpse of his eyes and instantly looked away feeling a tad bit sorry for the aggravated tone to get his attention. Embarrassed at his slip from reality, he grabbed the bag and thanked her. Then he quickly pulled off, no longer hungry but somewhat relieved that he heard an answer to what caused the turmoil boiling in the place where honest love once dwelled, all in the chorus of a song. She couldn't have a heart and that is why the deceit was so easy and so trifling. That answer seemed to be enough right then because he had to snap out of it. He couldn't let Tina have so much control...like the control she had right then.

Chapter 12

Kyle was approaching graduation from his training course and ready to report to his first unit. His excitement concerning his future duties and responsibility were manifested in his work ethic and enthusiasm for his class work. He naturally had the makings of a leader and had the personality type that aimed to be a general officer one day. Thought he was excited for his future, he was deeply concerned about the state of mind of his former roommate. Through Rodney he learned the continuing details of what had happened after the Tina incident. Numerous attempts to contact Jasper were made and he was starting to get worried about him. Jasper always seemed down more and more and distracted the few times that he did answer Kyle's phone calls.

Rodney shared this same growing concern and made it a point to stop by Jasper's apartment either before or after a gig at Jo Jo's. Rodney was the kind of guy that was quite persuasive at getting someone to talk. Whether it was his sheer muscular bulk or his optimistic personality seasoned with the ability to outtalk anyone, he had little trouble getting a response out of people. There was once a time when he and Jasper would talk about anything, lately Jasper had become somewhat distant and sometimes angry. The visits to Jasper's apartment were disheartening because it was once orderly compared to the cluttered disarray it had become. It was as if Jasper just didn't care and was trapped in a mindless routine of life; go to work, go home, and do nothing else.

One particular day the red flag for the roomies to take action was thrown. Kyle called Rodney one Sunday afternoon stating that he just spoke to Tina. "Bruh, that chic just called me talking about she will have to show Jasper that they belong together if I didn't convince him."

Rodney was playing with his infant daughter at the time, but that didn't stop his explosive reaction. "What the fuck does that mean? That bitch is crazy!" He looked up, saw Katrina staring at him, and lowered his tone. "What do you think that she was talking about? Pimp, that mess sounds weird for her to come at you like that. Na-mean?"

"Yeah, I know. I called Jasper to holla at him, but he didn't pick up. When are you going back up that way?" Kyle was coming up on the last days before graduation and planned to visit his folks in Georgia before reporting to his duty station. He was thinking about modifying those plans if he needed to.

"Man, I ain't got another show for two weeks from now. He probably ain't going to answer for me either." The annoyance rising in him, he continued forgetting that his wife was in the room, "Do I need to go talk to that bougie bitch? I heard that she lives around here somewhere now." Katrina sucked her teeth and he apologized, "Sorry baby."

"Brother, I don't know. That was bizarre for her to call me, because she knows that I can't stand her ass." The two continued their conversation in which Rodney promised to see about his homeboy in the next couple of days. He didn't tell Kyle that he was going to put a few feelers in the street to see what Tina was up to, and Tim as well, in case he was involved. For his sake, Rodney hoped that he wasn't.

Tina smiled as she hoped that her theatrical performance on the telephone with Kyle was enough to convince Jasper to at least call her to see what the fuss was about. She had taken her mom's advice and was going to fight to get back in Jasper's life. All she needed was a few moments of his time to convince him that it was a mistake and that they were meant to be together. He never answered her phone calls, so she decided to take things up a notch by contacting his friend. She knew that Kyle didn't like her but wouldn't rest until he investigated why she called him crying and carrying on angrily. It may be enough to spur an irate call from Jasper, she told herself, and she would have the chance to convince him to let her come over just once. All she needed was one face-to-face interaction, in his place and in his bed to make him remember that he still loved her, she told herself.

A couple of days passed without the expected response that she sought. Kyle didn't even call back to ask more questions or say something like, "He doesn't want to talk to you." She had envisioned how the night was going to be when she made love to him like never before after a little heated arguing. It seemed like that was not going to happen. Frustrated, she called Kyle....no answer. She called Jasper....no answer. She started to call Rodney and hung up before the phone rang.

Why doesn't he want to talk to me? She was thinking to herself many possible scenarios to why she was being ignored. She thought about the three buddies laughing at her. *I wonder if big booty Tara is fucking him again.* She envisioned Jasper with Tara and some of the other women that he was rumored to be with during college. Regardless of why, she felt that she had to do more to get his attention. The talking and crying didn't seem to help. She thought of her mother saying, "You have to do what you have to do..." over and over again.

Her plan had failed. Her eyes misted during her irrational mental search for a solution that may not be. She cursed Tim out loud for approaching her with money for intercourse. She cursed her parents for not giving her more money, and her dad specifically, for failing to stand up to her mom about it. She cursed the economy. She cursed and cursed until she focused on her mother saying, "If you want your man…" She wanted Jasper back terribly and felt that she could come up with some way of getting him back. Sitting in her sorority sister's spare bedroom she contemplated feasibilities. She eventually gave up so she could get ready for bed. She had an interview the next day.

Somewhere in the same city, the woman that was before Tina was sitting in her apartment contemplating on whether Jasper was deserving of a call from her. Tara had heard of Jasper's split from Tina through gossip soaring around the city of Pembrook. Her turmoil was whether she should see the breakup as an opportunity for a second chance or as karma for dumping her in the first place.

When someone is going through any type of ordeal, it seems like the world pays attention and offers its own commentary. Billboards suddenly seem to display something related to a person's thoughts. Every other commercial on television seems to subject one's situation. Sitcoms and talk shows tend to be about the same scenarios that have currently captured the mind. This was the case as Jasper sat alone in the dark sipping on some wine that had been in the fridge for a long time. He had ignored phone calls from Tina, his homeboys, his parents, and anyone that may inquire about what was going on with his love life.

As he flipped channels, one channel broadcasted a popular evangelist energetically soliciting those who were "sad, lost, or simply tired" to call in and request some type of prayer cloth package guaranteed to "sooth the depths of your troubles". Even ESPN was showing a weekly wrap-up of the week in sports news and happened to have two sportscasters arguing about a player from the Atlanta Hawks that was cheating on his team as he sought offers from other teams since he would be a free agent soon. As he continued his channel surfing, he finally landed on BET where some new late night show had so-called relationship experts and known comedians discussing the controversial topic of the differences between men and women. The host was constantly egging on both sides with his comments.

One passionate comedian was stumbling over his words in a retort to a female relationship counselor from New York. He stated, "It is in a female's nature to be sneaky, low-down, never satisfied, and trifling. Just look at Eve in the Bible." The audience was mixed with various pitches of laughter and booing. He paused to soak in his reactions and continued, "When a decent man is a victim to these low-down chicks, it hurts. That is why some men will remain dogs…" The overly afro-centric cutie on the panel, who was a self-proclaimed advisor for adult relationship enhancement and shamelessly plugging her new book jumped in with, "You are so wrong!" The comedian didn't even acknowledge the angry author with the high, bronze-colored afro as he continued, "...and that is eventually when good men go bad."

Jasper laughed out loud and said, "Amen, brother!" The rest of the conversation between the feuding sides on the TV kind of blurred after that. The mixture of wine and the recollection of his recent reality suddenly stung him to an emotional state close to bringing tears. The comedian had preached what seemed like truth to his soul right then. Jasper felt that deep down he was what most would consider a good guy in today's society. Educated, good job, no crime record, single (newly single), full of good intentions and had a good heart. He was now starting to lose the struggle to not be the stereotypical dog that was being discussed on TV at the moment.

"It is in a man's nature to want to hunt, control, and conquer regardless of how fine a woman he had," a caller into the show stated sounding like he was quite angry during his comment. The word fine was stressed. "Hell, I would probably cheat on Janet Jackson, if her fine ass was mine!" The word ass was bleeped out on the prerecorded show. The laughter and murmur of comments from the audience was too random to be generated by one of those applause machines that some shows were known to use.

Jasper was amidst his own recollections of past exploits. He was mentally fast forwarding and rewinding through some of the highlights of his young, yet broad dating experience. Dating may not be the most accurate word to illustrate the coming of age encounters that a lot of young men go through in order to find or define themselves, inflate their masculine significance, or just happen to fall into. Remembering some of the lame and clever lines he used to introduce himself to some women or make them smile made him grin. He thought about what he said to Tina, what he once said to Tara, and others. The talk show eventually ended unknown to Jasper who now was categorizing his mental rolodex of past and possible women into who would be eager for his attention, untouchable due to circumstances, and not worth the trouble.

Sometimes women don't fully understand the hold that they could potentially have on a man. This is especially true for the woman that is loved by a man that has been devastated by a haunting and hurting past, but has since overcome to give love to someone who eventually takes an already fragile heart and shatters it to even more forlorn fragments. This is also true for the woman who has a man that has graduated from the immature and childish ways of a doggish youth, just to put him back on the block again trying to study and search for the way to recover once again or how to return to the trifling games that he once gave up for a chance at true love. Jasper was in the latter situation. He could easily open the floodgates to numerous possible suitors, new ex's, or booty calls. The confusion that stirred in him and would soon lead him to some sleepless nights and deciding which type of guy he wanted to be: doleful lover boy or detached dog, lustful mack daddy or love maker. It was too easy for him to become the old version of himself; frat boy gripping all that he desired, but that part of his soul was tired, so tired. Even at such a young age he was both blessed and cursed to be a part of many women's daydreams, wishes, and prayers as well as a source of drama, wounds, and plights for many others. He wanted so badly to fight back the urge to act completely reckless and uncaring, but the loneliness that now planted itself in the hole gorged in his heart wanted to be held until it dissipated, even if temporarily…even if only for one night.

Sleep gradually overcame his slouched and tipsy body on the couch gripping one of the pillows on his firm and lonely couch while losing his grip on the glass that now only held a drop or two of fluid that accentuated the state he was in. If one could have read his last thoughts before he slipped into an exhausted and heartrending sleep, they would see that he settled the debate in his head, in which the panel from the talk show argued seemingly for him. He was going to embrace his past ways for a while. He knew that he would never be the dog that some talked about, but it was time to have some fun regardless of the shallow and selfish dealings due to come. He played new mind movies of things like presenting pancakes to beautiful women still laying sleepily and nude in his bed after nights of intense and validating sex episodes and the drama-filled phone calls that may follow after he intentionally failed to call them two weeks later.

Chapter 13

That weekend was sort of rough for Jasper. A lot of sleeping, a lot of drinking, and a lot of thinking filled the hours. His overactive mind kept replaying the events from that day of exposure, truth, and pain. Tina calling and leaving voice messages didn't help his dilemma of getting over it. He never answered, but he saved each of the voicemails to play later. It was as if each call was motivation to move on and also dragged him back into a fit of anger and sadness. He texted a few women from his past and entertained some of the "How are you doing?" phone calls from past admirers. He expected Tara to contact him, but he couldn't get himself to contact her.

The following Monday Jasper felt somewhat like a new man. He at least appeared to be one on the outside. He was more chipper at work as he completed work orders and answered his phone. Shelia noticed and so did Rick as well. Rick's typical side comments seemed to roll off of him instead of annoying him. Shelia was getting more aggressive, yet more subtle at the same time with her flirtatious innuendos. A few times Jasper responded with a wink or a sly comment like, "You ain't ready for that." He had no intention of doing anything with someone at his place of employment. His dad always used to say a phrase that went something like, "You don't ever eat where you shit" or "You don't shit where you lay." Something like that…

Rodney and Kyle still weren't fooled. You hang around someone for long enough, you learn their coping mechanisms. The sense of detachment and nonchalance exhibited by their friend only showed that he either was not into Tina as much as he thought or that he was soon going to rampage on the hearts and bodies of other women to fill the void that Tina dug out in his heart. Kyle always worried more than his roommates while Rodney was always the most relaxed about situations. During one of their weekly lunch time phone calls Rodney told him, "Check this out. I know exactly what he needs, bruh. I'ma hook him up with the singer in my band. He needs a nice older woman to get his mind right. Know what I'm saying? You feel me? She was asking about getting a piece of him anyway."

Kyle could only laugh. "Whatever, man. Whatever." He knew how much of a ladies' man Jasper had always been. He knew that Jasper would be alright.

A couple of days later, Jasper finally picked up Rodney's call and accepted a VIP ticket to attended his next show at Jo Jo's.

He needed to get out and enjoy his changed relationship status. He felt conflicted, but ok for the rest of the week. The excitement of hanging at the club was mixed with fear that his ex may show up there. The downturn of his attitude was an incident at work. Rick noticed his protégé reading an email from who he thought was his girlfriend. His usual take-stuff-too-far nature kicked in.

"I noticed that was a little love email from your Tina. So when do we get the pleasure of meeting her, Jap." Jasper only closed the webpage and rolled his eyes. He remembered what Jasper said in the hallway during their confrontation, but he wanted to push Jasper's buttons anyway. Rick continued, "You should let her get a tour of the building sometime. You know… show her what you do." He gave his supervisor a look that screamed, *Please leave me alone!*

"Sir, I don't think she will be coming around here for a while." Not trying to get Rick to ask what that meant and to get him further from the trail of suspecting any inappropriate relationship with Shelia, he just lied and said, "She umm….works a lot of hours during the week." The fact that he had to lie further pushed his level of anger after reading the email from Tina that stated "We will be together again. You will see!"

If the facial expression of Jasper didn't tell him to back off while Rick was talking, his abrupt departure from his desk should have sparked something. It didn't. Rick kept talking to his back as he walked toward the door, "Oh, you two must be having some type of love spat. Trust me! Women just aren't worth it, man! Trust me."

Sometimes a person has to win a bunch of minor battles in the war of getting over someone. Something as small and routine as washing the sheets, in which two bodies once laid and played in, is a little victory in moving on. One thing that Jasper did was go to Tina's favorite snow cone stand alone and order himself her favorite flavor early that Saturday afternoon. His heart was beating as if he finished running a few miles while he stood in line and ordered.

He missed her, no doubt. As he tasted the first scoop of the frozen reminder of a love once shared, he looked at his phone and almost called her. The torture became easier with each taste as he remembered the sweetness that he once shared, and as the cup emptied, it symbolized that the same sweetness was going to be gone soon and couldn't come back. As he slurped up the bottom of melted ice and sugary fluid, he noticed the other flavors on the wall in the little stand. A thought came to him. If he wanted to, he could decide to get up and try another flavor, never having to taste Tina's ever again; he only had to get back in line. He did just that, and ordered something different, more exotic. It was definitely time to move on. Funny, he kept the empty first cup for a day as a small trophy for winning the next battle. He promised himself that he would throw it away on his way to work Monday.

He completed his typical Saturday routine and took a nap before he got ready to enjoy Rodney's show at Jo Jo's. He starched up his jeans, like Kyle always used to do to his, heavily to make a definite crease. He laid out his jewelry and cologne before making a pre-event drink and hopping in the shower. He did about fifty pushups attempting to make his chest look a little more pumped up. He was ready to make his presence felt to the world. He found some of Tina's old hair spray under the sink and threw it away without blinking. "Fuck her." Minutes later, he was on his way to the club.

Traffic on that particular Saturday night was surprisingly light, and he made it to Beale Street fairly quickly. Sonya greeted him at the door and brought him over to the VIP section. The other band members and the owner of the club greeted Jasper. Rodney hugged his homeboy, paused, and then looked toward Sonya. He looked back at his homeboy and said, "Umm huh." Those two words and that look said volumes in an unspoken way which basically meant, *She has been asking about you and wants to see what's up. I think that you should entertain that because she is definitely down for whatever. I think you will not be disappointed by the experience, so I strongly recommend that you should pursue.*

Jasper acknowledged back with a shocked look, "Umm huh?" which meant, *Really? Since you brought that to my attention, and it meets your approval, I will definitely pursue that opportunity. Thanks for the heads up!*

Dipped in Soul gave a mesmeric sold-out performance that kept the patrons, the owners, and the bartenders very entertained and contented. It was obvious that Rodney had an influence on the band as more bass guitar loaded songs were being played in the set than before. Sonya eyed Jasper throughout the night and sat by him during every break. Jasper was turned on by the seductive soul singer. He felt like his old self as cute, flirtatious words spewed from him to her with ease. He enjoyed older women, and she was close to Shelia's age. It undeniably started to look like Rodney was right when Sonya grabbed his leg before her final set and said, "Make sure you don't go home without me."

It didn't take long for the band to break down and load their equipment after the final song of the night. Shortly thereafter, Sonya and Jasper were pulling up to his apartment. He did a quick scan of the parking lot as he opened his door for Tina's car and he led the songstress upstairs. Instantly, she dropped her dress and asked for a towel to take a quick shower. Jasper kept his composure as he looked over the beauty and gazed into her horny, hungry eyes. She walked in the bathroom and looked back with a smile. The water started as Jasper made a couple of drinks and turned on the TV. He was glad that he decided to clean up his place earlier though he wasn't expecting late-night company.

His heart was beating with anticipation and nervousness because he didn't want to not look like a boy in front of the grown woman. He took a gamble that she left the door open on purpose. He threw his clothes in the corner and rushed in, his dick already throbbing. "Damn, you got a six pack!" blurted from the mouth of the naked and wet woman standing in the shower as Jasper stepped in. "I see that you caught my hint and decided to join me." Jasper could only smile as he eyed the soap rinsing off of her. She said, "I see that another part of you caught my hint too, sweetie."

She was unlike Tina in many ways. She had the type of thickness that time pleasantly developed and the type of confidence that shame couldn't ever hinder. His hands grasped sheer beauty as the warm water sprayed them. He wanted to take her right there in the shower, but she slowed his advances. "Hold on, sweetie. Don't want you to get it before I give you a lil something." They groped, kissed, and played in the shower until the water started to become cold. They dried off quickly and went to the bed.

Some say that with age, comes experience. Jasper was hoping that statement to be true and applied to his situation right then. She sat him down and instantly grabbed him below and starting pleasing him skillfully with her lips, tongue, and hands.

Jasper was concentrating so hard on not ejaculating quickly, but Sonya was intent on getting him to that point. *Man, Tina never did it like this!* was his last thoughts before letting go without warning Sonya. She simply smiled and said, "Good. Now that we got that one out of the way, let's take a quick nap before I break you off like I promised earlier." In response, Jasper could only let out, "Oh shit! Ok," between trying to catch his breath.

Shortly after Jasper dozed off, he was aggressively awakened and Sonya kept her promise. They finally went to sleep as the sun was coming up. Satisfied, Jasper kissed her on the forehead and gave her a quick squeeze before she rolled over and slept in his arms.

Sonya was hardened by years of sleeping with various men, whether they were married or not, some who cared or broke her heart. There were some who used her while others adored her. She was tired of the hurt, but not the thrill. She smiled as she reminisced. Years ago, she would have loved to have had a man as sweet as Jasper and she truly enjoyed sleeping with him. She knew that she would only break his heart if they got together too many times. She woke him up a few hours later and said, "One day, you are going to make someone very happy." Then she proceeded to put on her clothes. She knew that the young man in bed was laying there in need and fighting his pride to say so. She banked on that and headed toward the door. "Come lock the door behind me." Nude, he walked behind her, both wanting to say something, and both of them wanted to not seem weird. "Call me sometime, sweetie", were her last words before she turned to walk to her car.

He sat on his couch nude, tipsy, and bewildered. He mentally slapped himself for acting like a wimp with Sonya. He used to be better at "slanging and banging" women as one of his frat brothers used to say. He was so taken aback that he felt anger all of a sudden. He was angry at Tina for putting him back in the dating game like that so suddenly. He was angry that he would have to endure more women like Sonya and Tina before he found true love. He was angry that he has to either play or be played in the so-called boy-girl game. He was angry that he was even thinking about love at that moment.

The boy-girl game was exactly that, a game. The rules and game play should be simple, and he simply wanted to win. Jasper rolled the dice and his match went like this. Boy meets girl. Boy likes girl. Boy dates girl. Boy has to keep his feelings in check (at first), yet let girl know how he feels (not too soon). Boy likes girl even more. Boy has to trust her, but keep one eye open as he never knows when she might do wrong. Boy dates other girls (at the same time) and hopes to not get caught. Boy likes girl more than anyone. Boy has to get rid of the other girls so he can focus on girl. Boy puts his all into girl. Boy ends up hurt. Boy ends up alone.

Game over? Not really. Jasper would pick up the dice again and proceed to get more turns, per se. So…Boy goes back to dating other girls, until he gets back to "Boy likes girl". He hoped the next ending would be different. Until then, the game had to move on. He laughed at his almost amateur reintroduction to dating. He promised that he wouldn't let it happen again. He finished the drink that he made when he first got home and never got to since it was sitting on the counter. Afterwards, he went back to his bedroom and laid in his bed still naked.

Later, he woke up and drank a big cup of water before working out and taking a shower. Afterwards, he eyed the drink that he made for Sonya, which was watered down and downed it. He grabbed his phone which had a battery that was close to being dead, and checked his text messages and voicemails. The only voicemail he had was from Rodney who was curious about how the night went with Sonya. He had two text messages, one from Tina that simply said, "Hi" and one from Sonya saying that she made it home and that she would be in contact for round two soon.

Later, he started to pack his bags for the upcoming ProtectCon trip. He eventually called Rodney back and confirmed that he did indeed hook up with Sonya. "That's what's up, lil playa! I knew that you would do it 13-O-2 style!" Rodney was referring to the good times that they used to have when they were roommates. Later in the conversation Rodney hesitated as he knew that what he was about to bring up at that point may change the whole mood. "Hey, ummm....I got a phone call from your ex, Tina. She was damn near begging me to talk to her. When she called I almost hung up on her ass, but ummm....something ain't right with her, mane! She called Kyle not too long ago, too."

Jasper could only hold the phone. His thoughts raced with wonderment, curiosity, and anger at the same time. Calling his old roommates was showing that she was desperate. Tina and Kyle couldn't stand each other, *so why would she call him?*

Chapter 14

There is something about being in Washington, D.C. that pulls on one's patriotism and tickles one's sense of history. As Jasper, Shelia, and two other coworkers rode from the Baltimore-Washington International Airport to their hotel in Arlington, Virginia he was in awe at seeing the monuments and historic sites that he had learned about in school years ago. Shelia paid the driver of the van a little extra to take the scenic route that she knew the others would enjoy. She had been there several times and knew the others were rookies to the area.

The others were excited, but Shelia was visibly nervous as she continuously scribbled notes into a notebook. She was asked to present at the last minute on behalf of the company and she wanted to make a good impression. She wasn't even scheduled to go, but her supervisor couldn't make it due to a family emergency and decided to send her. The four of them were going to divide up the sessions and give a brief report about them when they returned.

Jasper was kind of nervous himself because he found himself looking at Shelia differently. For the trip, she wasn't wearing her typical business attire. She wore a simple nylon jogging suit and an alumni t-shirt from her alma mater. Seeing her in more relaxed clothing and in a more relaxed atmosphere made her more attractive, more authentic. She was too busy to notice the occasional glance from him. Jasper wondered if she would try anything during the trip. They were fortunate to all have their own rooms, and he entertained the idea in his head. *Man, get your shit straight. You can't fuck her....that's your bosses' boss....bad business.* He looked on with the others at the sights of the city attempting to shake the thought.

Shortly thereafter, the representatives from InfoTech Solutions arrived at their hotel and checked in. Shelia suggested that they go to dinner after they settled in and verify their itineraries. Shelia looked over Jasper's shoulder and noticed that he was in room 703. "Cool. I'm just down the hall from you in room 710," Shelia stated. Jasper looked around to see if the other attendees from the company were around, and boldly stated, "Cool. I know where to come find you later if I need something, Ms. Bunton." He stressed the word come intentionally but threw in the last part to make it sound somewhat legitimate. Shocked, Shelia could only say, "Ok," and turned toward the elevator.

In a different time zone, Tina was enacting the first part of her plan to get her man back. Due to Jasper's oversight, Tina's name was still on the apartment lease. She waited until he left and decided that she was going to claim to have lost her key while Jasper was at the conference. The office manager recalled not seeing her around much and questioned her guardedly. He was an older gentleman that had a strong affinity for some of the young black women in the apartment complex. "So you say that he is out of town, huh?"

She saw that her story was failing fast and started crying instantly. She cried and concocted a story that was so believable that he gave her a spare key and even waived the $50 lockout fee. To add some extra sugar to the end of the story, she gave him a solid hug and she said, "Thanks sir!" The apartment manager was visibly flustered and felt a sense of pride for being able to help out a beautiful woman.

Elated, she had a smirk on her face as she got ready to go into part two of her plan, which was to check out his apartment to see if there were any clues of another female's presence. She turned the key given to her and paused before entering. She was joyful that she didn't see anything that led her to believe that another female replaced her. She carried a bag with candles, lingerie, a couple of shirts, and some other items. She originally planned on setting up the apartment with these items and being present when he returned home, but she had no idea when he would return. She was slyly trying to pry that info from Rodney or Jasper, if he ever answered the phone. She now had the bag packed in case she gained any information about his return and needed to act fast. Without that, she purposely did not set up anything and would wait. She did place one of her t-shirts in the back of the closet as bait to get him to perhaps let her in to get it back.

Later that evening as Tina was leaving Jasper's apartment in Tennessee and Jasper was having dinner with Shelia and other coworkers in Virginia, DeMarcus was in Arkansas hoping to consummate his relationship with Tara. Starting off with a few occasional conversations, Tara and DeMarcus began to hang out from time to time. Despite his attempts for more, he was always rejected when it came to someone going over the other's house or spending the night together.

Tara debated on whether to give DeMarcus any attention and turned him down plenty of times. One lonely night after looking through some old pictures of her and Jasper, she simply stated, "Fuck it!" and picked up the phone to give DeMarcus a chance to hang out, but with restrictions. "Um, we can go to the movies or something, but that's it." DeMarcus quickly agreed as he tried to be cool and subdue the surprise he felt.

He noticed that she suddenly seemed so available to him as if she was trying to get back at Jasper or simply hoping that getting close to DeMarcus would get her close to Jasper. She eventually revealed that she missed Jasper. This pissed DeMarcus off, but he was going to selfishly try to indulge himself as long as he could. He was hoping that Jasper would be out of the picture by then. He was going to play on that fact until she got caught up and slept with him. He wanted her so badly, almost to the point of madness.

That night she called him to vent about class and discuss random stuff. His thoughts instantly became dirty, and he got an erection thinking about getting a chance with the short, country talking object of his affection. He quickly asked, "Why don't you stop by for a second? I was going to cook a few hamburgers and watch a lil TV. You should come through tonight."

Tara hesitated and said, "Well, I dunno. Maybe that is not a good idea right now." Her last sexual experience was earlier in the summer and wasn't an exciting one. She felt susceptible to seduction and wasn't exactly trying to squelch it. She thought about Jasper, her loneliness, her bedroom boredom, and DeMarcus' persistence. As if reading her mind, DeMarcus said, "You know you want to. Come on through. Do you like mayo and ketchup on yours?"

Still hesitant, Tara eventually replied with an inaudible "Fuck it!" Then she said into the phone, "Ok, make my burger a big one. Some of us ain't afraid to feed their hips!"

DeMarcus managed to play it cool though his facial expression was a mixture of shock and delight. They solidified a time, and DeMarcus ended the conversation with, "Cool, I will see you soon." It was set and both of them knew deep down the possibilities that hanging out may bring. DeMarcus let out a yelp when he hung up the phone then went to his bedroom to relieve his unexpected excitement and get ready.

Chapter 15

The conference was going well for Jasper. He learned who some of the top players were in the government and private sector concerning networking and security. He posed for pictures with hackers and CEOs of software companies. He revisited several booths set up by vendors advertising their services over and over again in order to get the freebies like footballs and coffee mugs imprinted with logos.

The weeklong conference never got boring to him. His coworkers that accompanied him didn't seem to share his enthusiasm. During one of the breakout sessions, Shelia sat by Jasper and asked how much he was enjoying the conference. Maybe it was her way of breaking the newfound sexual tension that was building or perhaps she was simply playing her role as senior leadership. During their conversation, she threw a few ideas at him concerning how she should give her presentation that was scheduled for that Friday. They talked about network security as well as random subjects like Rick and his accusations. She revealed to him that Rick honestly thought that it was partly racially motivated that Jasper and Sheila both went to ProtectCon and almost got written up for insubordination. They laughed, and she genuinely gave advice and mentorship. It struck Jasper as strange that she didn't come on to him at all during the chat.

As she was mentioning that the InfoTech crew should have dinner together later, Jasper's cell phone buzzed due to his receipt of a text message from Tina. She sent at least two a day saying trouble-free messages like "Hi" or "Have a good night". This particular text propelled him into a tailspin of emotions, and Shelia caught the change in countenance. "Hey, ummm, Mr. Hooks.....are you ok?" Jasper took the question as an opportunity to plant a seed of desire and inquiry to his superior.

"Well Ms. Bunton, my ex-girlfriend has been bugging me lately. I told her that it was over, but she just won't leave a brother alone." He looked her dead in the eyes for a reaction in which Shelia responded like he knew she would...like he hoped she would.

"Well, that ex-girlfriend of yours must be missing the fine, chocolate brother that she used to have. Now she doesn't know how to act. Sugar, her lost will be someone else's gain." Jasper noticed how the R's rolled more than usual and how her posture straightened as she said those words. It was clear that Jasper was at that moment opening up compared to his usual repulsion of her advances. Jasper was about to hit her with another cliché line, but he noticed one of the executives from another company walking up to them to steal a moment of Shelia's time, probably in the attempt to sell a product. Jasper took the circumstance as a sign that he was heading into forbidden territory and sat back in his chair. The gentleman introduced himself as a representative of a company that was seeking a joint venture with InfoTech Solutions. With a quick, quasi-authentic chortle, Shelia was back into professional mode and walked away with the executive to hear what he had to say.

The conversation Jasper had with Shelia was still reeling in his head for the rest of that day. He mindlessly went through the rest of the sessions that were basically workshops and meetings where a lot of brainy people with good ideas told of new questions in which there were no true answers. Though he was learning a lot, he felt that the conference was for the managerial types, not the entry level employees of the world like him. Nonetheless, he felt that the exposure was motivating and somewhat eye-opening.

He didn't see Shelia for the rest of the day. One of the younger attendees from another corporation caught his eye a couple of times. He was looking forward to making a play at getting her attention here and there, but some lavishly dressed guy seemed to always pop up every time he looked at her too long. *Ol' Captain Save-a-Hoe muthafucka!,* was his initial thought. *He sees me looking and is straight up blocking. Ol' punk muthafucka.* At that point, he decided to stop his contemplation about pursuing the cute stranger with only two days left of the conference. He thought about how sex with Shelia would be and smiled. *Maybe I will see later.*

Suddenly his phone buzzed with a text message from one of his favorite fraternity brothers, DeMarcus. He assumed that he was sending a message about what happened with Tim. It was only a matter of time before everyone would find out what he and Tina did. It simply stated, "You were on my mind, bruh. How are you doing?" He hadn't heard from DeMarcus since graduation and texted back, "Man, I'm just at this conference trying not to get in trouble. You know how I do, man?"

DeMarcus was sitting, next to a napping Tara, in his bedroom grinning and trying not to laugh out loud. For the second time, he felt the softness of her breasts and thighs as he indulged himself in the pleasures that she offered. She stopped by after her morning class to continue what they did the night before.

The prior night he did get his wish as she felt comfortable enough to stay the night. He was such a gentleman offering her his bed as he slept on the couch when she started drifting off. He waited until she was good and snoring softly. Then he patiently loosened her clothing and rather aggressively rubbed and grouped her until her inhibitions loosened as she woke up. Without waiting, he entered her as soon as he felt that he had the green light and was enjoying himself too much to stop once he started moving. He enjoyed himself a little too much as he finally got what he wanted and prematurely ended the episode.

She came back by his place to finish what they had started and to receive some stimulation while she was actually fully aware of what was happening. As she slept, DeMarcus couldn't help contacting Jasper as a way of saying to him, *I got you. I am winning this time*, but his typed words were more of a gesture of hello. DeMarcus felt that Jasper would find out one day that he had slept with Tara, but he didn't care even though he knew that Jasper probably would.

He looked at the solidly built frame of the woman in his bed lying without panties. He congratulated himself by slapping her on the ass to wake her up. As she stirred and said, "What's up?", another text from Jasper chimed in on DeMarcus's cell phone saying, "I know you are handling your business back in Pembrook, frat." He couldn't control his smile as he replied to Tara verbally yet answering Jasper's text, "You just don't know…..you just don't know."

At the ProtectCon convention, the last meeting Shelia had to attend for the day was about to conclude. Her eyes had started to glaze over from hearing the dry monotone voice of the presenter and after a larger than normal lunch that was arranged by one of the sponsoring entities. Earlier, she had thought it was cute that Jasper seemed to have been flirting with her. Maybe it was more fun to her when she was doing the flirting for suddenly it seemed kind of odd. Like Jasper, she had been eyeing a few possible people to hook up with before they all departed on Saturday. A lot of flirtation came her way from gentlemen of many shapes, sizes, and races since the beginning of the convention as well as one woman.

As the last question and answer portion of the day finally ended, she shot up quickly to meet up with the others from InfoTech Solutions to check on them. She was looking forward to relaxing and going over her presentation a little bit before meeting them for dinner later that evening. She walked out of the main conference room and saw them all sitting at a table near the balcony enjoying some of the snacks and coffee that was laid out by the employees of the conference center.

"Okay everyone. I hope you had a long, interesting day. Let's walk back to our hotel and chill until about 7:30. Meet me in the lobby, and we can walk to the Italian restaurant that Phil wanted to check out." At that point, all four of them gathered their things and walked back to where they were staying not saying much. Jasper and Shelia both didn't even regard each other much.

Right before 6 p.m., Jasper was sitting in his room restless. He tried to take a nap, but he had a dream about Shelia during the short time he was able to rest. His dream started off with Sonya giving him some head and singing the Stephanie Mills version of "If I Were Your Woman" while she was riding his dick. Somewhere in the dream, Shelia popped up singing the original, older version that was sung by Gladys Knight and the Pips replacing Sonya on top of him. Jasper woke up thinking about why he was so attracted to older women and was amused by his dream.

He got dressed early and was going to go to the bar near the lobby and have a drink before meeting with the others. As he headed to the elevator, he passed by room 710. He paused for about half a minute and doubled back. He felt himself starting to sweat as he raised his fist to knock on Shelia's hotel room door. Again he paused, thinking, *Why am I doing this?* He thought of several instances that she hinted inappropriate things to him at work. *If this doesn't work out, this is going to be embarrassing.* With that last thought, he moved the fist suspended in the air and knocked on her door. He thought about running when she answered the door still in her clothes from earlier, and her face was plastered with an expression of surprise and question.

"Yes, Mr. Hooks? Is everything ok?" Shelia was totally caught off guard and was just about to take off her clothes and jump in the shower. She had just finished ironing a blouse that she wanted to wear that evening. She looked Jasper in the eye waiting for a response. She noticed that his mouth was open on the verge of saying something that seemed to get caught. He blinked, took a deep breath and began to try again to speak when the chime from the elevator sounded. Without thinking, Jasper jumped in her room and closed the door. Too late to turn away.

Shelia thought that his actions were charming and guessed at his intent. To break the silence, she turned to offer him a drink. She always bought a small bottle of tequila before going on a business trip. This kept her from buying too many overpriced drinks at the bar or from opening the little bottles that sometimes come with a room the same caliber that she was staying in for the conference. "Mr. Hooks….", were the only words that she got out before feeling his youthful hands around her waist. He was slowly pulling her to him and then kissed the back of her neck. Delightfully thrilled and shocked, Shelia did not move.

Jasper had passed the point of no return. The undercover and illegal flirtations had finally led to what he they both wanted. They wanted it for different reasons, but with the same objective. That was to receive and give pleasure to the other with no shame or risk of getting caught. He gripped her bottom and was shocked at how firm it was. She gripped his hands which were gripping her and moved them up toward the buttons holding her skirt up. Slowly he popped open the four buttons while his lips never left her neck. She moaned and stepped forward allowing the skirt to drop to her feet. She stood there in the somewhat dark room only lit with one lamp in a corner and a little light emanating from the partially closed bathroom. Jasper took a moment to marvel how flawless her ass was. It was shapely, yet well-toned and had no stretch marks at all.

Sheila felt his eyes take her in. She suddenly spun around and started unbuttoning her white shirt. Jasper stood in place not wanting to be too aggressive or too passive at the same time. She spoke, "So Mr. Hooks, it seems like you want some of this candy that I want to give you." Jasper still was stationary as he was thinking, *Damn, I never thought her body was that banging.* As she unhooked her bra, she continued, "Well, take off your clothes, little boy, because I got some sweetness for you."

Jasper grabbed himself and whispered, "Hell yeah." His hesitation died then and his ravenous needs boosted his confidence as he walked to her and pinched her ass. He kissed her neck again before darting to her lips. He thought about Tina, he thought about Sonya. He felt an excitement that was foreign to him as he began to lead his supervisor to her unmade bed. The twinge of doing something forbidden mixed well with his curiosity and temptation, because he knew that he had to keep this a secret from everyone. As their lips and tongues explored each other almost roughly, he was happy that he took a chance and knocked on that door.

Minutes later, they were both laying in the room's king size bed completely naked and rolling amongst the numerous pillows. Shelia withdrew her struggle against the vascular arms of Jasper's, and he ended up on top of her. "Hey baby....do me a favor and turn off the bathroom light and grab a couple of condoms from my accessories bag in there." He did as asked and Shelia said to him as he returned, "I'm glad that I brought some. I'm glad that you want some of this candy, little boy." Jasper unconsciously shuddered at hearing the words "little boy" for the third time.

Jasper pulled one from the wrapper and thought to himself, *I just have to feel this before I put this condom on.* He plunged inside of Shelia then pulled out. *Man that shit was tight as hell. It must've been a while for her.* Shelia's gazed upon the young man hovering over her with passionate submission and a yearning for more. He covered up his dick and plunged inside again moving slowly and slightly increasing the speed of his stroke as he went on. He was still in disbelief at what was transpiring. He was having sex with a woman that had the baddest body that he had ever seen and she was in his supervisory chain at work.

Shelia was probably enjoying it more than the one on top of her. It had indeed been a few months since she was pleasured by a man. She had a few bedside fantasies at home while playing with her toys thinking about Jasper ever since he walked through the InfoTech Solutions lobby. Half an hour later, he was still thrusting with a pretty steady and intense momentum. She was in sheer wonderment for some of her last adventures did not last that long, and it seemed like he wasn't going to let up or tire anytime soon. As she was about to cum a second time, she turned her head to the right to bite into the pillow and noticed that it was 7:10 p.m. on the alarm clock on the nightstand. As she started to think, *Oh shit, we are going to be late meeting the others*, a loud thunderous moan escaped her mouth validating again the contentment of her experience with Jasper.

After she caught her breath, she looked again at the alarm clock and the green LED lights blinked 7:19 p.m. Jasper was amped up and ready to keep going, but she stopped him and said, "Ummm, sugar. It's, umm, almost time for us to be downstairs." She started to bark orders as they hopped out of the bed. "First, flush that condom and use one of the extra towels in there to freshen yourself up. Then, I need you to go downstairs and let them know that I am finishing up my presentation for tomorrow, and that I will meet them downstairs by 8 p.m. Let them know that I saw you in the hallway on your way to the elevator and stopped you." She took a deep breath and finished with, "Finally, I need you to play it cool during dinner and promise me that you will give me some more of that sweet dick later."

Jasper silently smiled and did as instructed. He made it downstairs around 7:31.

During dinner, there was a silent awkwardness between Shelia and Jasper. None of the other co-workers and others that joined them were even slightly suspicious for the two had plenty of practice playing off any attraction to each other. They also never made eye contact throughout the night.

Jasper replayed the sex bout that he had earlier and was looking forward to round two after dinner. He didn't climax, and he desperately wanted to cap the evening doing so. He noticed how submissive she was during the act. Given the amount of time, missionary was the only position that they got to do. He recalled how tight the pussy was while he was in it. He assumed that she didn't get much male attention therefore explaining that fact. He was still shocked at how firm her body was. Though she was thirteen years older, he had seen a lot of women who had let themselves go at her age.

For the most part, dinner was uneventful. Each of the InfoTech Solutions employees gave mini-reports to Shelia, and she asked that all at the table attend the session that she had to present the next day. Shelia smoothly acted like she was not under Jasper only hours earlier. Jasper wrote in his memory that he might have a winner on his hand and a good piece that he could get from time to time.

After dinner, they were all walking back to the hotel and having random conversations while enjoying the city sites. Shelia stealthily moved next to the young protégée and said almost under her breath, "Ok, hotshot. When we get back to the hotel, leave your door open, and I will be there in 20 minutes. It's my turn now." Jasper was amazed at how smooth, yet potent, she was at that moment. Even the look in her eyes showed that she meant business. He felt that she was holding back earlier. He was simultaneously terrified and energized at what was to come.

Chapter 16

The next morning, a fatigued Jasper strolled over to the table in the lobby of the conference hall that offered coffee, hot tea, and breakfast treats full of sugar. Shelia had totally flipped it on Jasper when she got to his room. She brought him a drink and told him to drink it. She pushed him on the bed and said things like, "Pull your dick out, lil boy, and show me how much you want this candy." She touched, she teased, and she damn near tortured him in round after round of acrobatic and exhilarating sex. Then when it was all said and done, she got up, got dressed and said, "I am about to practice my presentation, Mr. Hooks. I will see you a lil later. Goodnight." He was definitely feeling the effects of his good time. He never imagined that she was so domineering and forceful in the bed.

She was to present at 10 a.m. on the subject "Keeping the Client Secure in a World of Budgets, Regulations, and Evolution". Jasper strolled in with his second cup of coffee and took a seat near the front with the others from his company. Shelia looked totally refreshed and ready to present, shockingly to Jasper after their rendezvous that ended merely eight hours prior. Promptly at

10 o'clock, a CEO from another company introduced Shelia and read off a short biography. In it, there were quite a few impressive credentials and projects under her belt that was notable for those in the information technology field. The gentleman concluded with, "Now, I present to you, Ms. Shelia Bunton."

Shortly after she began, one of the people a couple of seats over from Jasper made a statement to another fellow attendee about how she rolled the R's when she spoke. Suddenly, Shelia introduced him and asked him to give his feelings on working at a helpdesk. The two gossiping attendees were silently staring as he stood up and hoped that he didn't hear their conversation earlier. He wondered if it was a planned opportunity to introduce him to others in the field and help him stand out or if it was a way for her to "piss on his tree", as his father would say, in front of other female attendees. He stood up looking stunned and began to tell a little bit of his experience in the short period of time working at a helpdesk. He tried to keep it relevant to what his supervisor, and now playmate, was discussing. It was obvious that some of the audience members were stunned at how clearly and intelligently he spoke. Unfazed, he enjoyed his few moments of fame and sat down. Shelia thanked him and continued the presentation.

Later, after the end of the presentation, some people were staying around shaking hands and in their own conversations.

Jasper was sitting in his seat reading a text from Tina, when he was approached by a tall, Caucasian gentleman with a smile like a car salesman. "So how long have you been with InfoTech, young man?" Before he could reply, Shelia showed up and jumped in the conversation. "How are you doing, Brandon? How are things since you left the company last year?" One could see the embarrassment in the guy's face as it turned red. The way that Shelia said left, it made it seem like she used that word in place of something.

He simply replied with, "Hi Shelia. Nice presentation", before walking away.

Shelia looked at Jasper and said, "Vultures are everywhere and love to seek our young talent in the attempt to get an inside scoop on what we got going on. Be careful." Jasper never thought that a normal job would bring competition like that, but he was too new in the profession to know or understand.

His reply to her was, "Thanks, ma'am. So you wanna do the same tonight?" If Shelia's skin was fair, she would have visibly blushed.

Tina was back in Pembrook talking to her sorority sister, Vivian, during lunch at one of the soul food spots in town. She was telling her how much she missed Jasper and how he took care of her, inside and outside of the bedroom. "Girl, he would get this look in his eyes, and you knew that it was on! I miss that shit!" Vivian was tickled at how detailed her friend's conversation was. She knew Jasper, but never looked at him like that.

Vivian was all into the conversation listening to Tina's recount of how things went down with Tim on that life-changing day months ago. The rumors were everywhere with multiple versions changing more as they were retold. Vivian had heard that Tina was bored sexually with Jasper and that Tim was the replacement. She had no shame talking to the source and getting in on the gossip.

"Aw hell naw! Jasper was fucking King Ding-a-Ling compared to that sweating monster, Tim. Girl, I fucked up. I don't know why I even got into that shit. I was good, girl. Good man, taking care of me... and the bomb in bed. You feel me?" Vivian smiled. "I just got caught up in getting money and didn't want Jasper to reject me because I didn't have a job yet." She continued to tell Vivian how Tim approached her at a party the week of graduation and made a drunk and joking proposal about how he would pay for a woman like her.

Vivian, intently listening was internally calling her sister a hoe and recognizing how much she had messed up. She had heard stories about Jasper and her curiosity was suddenly sparked.

She had a cousin in Memphis, and she suddenly felt the urge (and a new reason) to travel that way for a visit. She made trips to Memphis often for work, and she was going to inquire about it when she got back to the office. Tina didn't fully understand that it is usually for the best for a female to keep her bedroom details to herself. You never know who might be listening or planning to experience what is told.

Rodney called Sonya to ensure she knew of the time change for practice with the band that day. "What up there, Sonya? You ready to do this today?"

Sonya was folding a load of clothes, and replied, "You said 6 o'clock, right? I will be there, boy. Is Will going to be there? He sounded iffy when I talked to him yesterday."

Will, the lead singer of Dipped in Soul, wasn't around as much as a leader of a band should be. The drummer suspected that he was working on trying to get a solo career and recording in a studio somewhere. Rodney angered by the possibility, and lack of Will's leadership, kept the group motivated and practicing for their steady gig at Jo Jo's. "Playa, I hope that fucker does right. He is the one that signed the muthafuckin' contract at Jo Jo's. He's the muthafuckin' bitch that told me how he needed a bass player to round out his all-star team. How the fuck…"

"Yo, yo, YO! You ain't mad at me, Rod. Calm down with that shit, bruh! If he ain't there, he ain't going to get his share of the bread. We know enough shit to put on a show and get this paper." Sonya always seemed to be the one that kept Rodney and Will from killing each other. Will seemed to be in the band for fame, women, and the money. Rodney loved music. He lived music therefore his passion came off as rage at times. To change the subject, she asked, "When does your cute buddy come back in town?"

Rodney's anger instantly calmed down and was replaced by hearty laughter. Jasper had told him how it all went down after she left the morning after they hooked up. Rodney listened to his sister in soul and finally said, "My boy said that you played him. Damn near said 'Thank you' and left his country ass a tip before you left." Sonya was embarrassed and knew that she was only trying to be tough and not get caught up. She was attracted to his kindness, his genuineness, and the enthusiasm he had during sex. She was so used to getting played that the thought of letting someone actually like her seemed foreign, seemed wrong.

She took a deep breath, and said, "Alright, bitch, whatever. Is he coming back from his trip soon? I didn't ask you for all of that." After a pause, she asked, "So do you know or what?"

Rodney did not know about Shelia nor did he hear anything else about Tina. He would have thought that Sonya was wrong for his homeboy any other time, but he felt that the two somehow needed each other, even if only for a little while. He just hoped that he would be spared any drama or had to be caught in the middle in case things went sour between the two. "Yeah he should be back this weekend. You should call him to put a bid in for his time. Ya feel me?"

She decided to do just that. "Yeah. I will hit him up…and I will see you at practice later, bighead." Her lips formed in a dazzlingly bright smile as they hung up.

Tara sat on her couch waiting on her next class in her bra and panties. It was a typical hot summer in Pembrook, and that was a typical act for students attempting to save money and keep from running the air conditioner constantly. She sat there staring at her phone as the fan noisily blew on her. She felt that she had made a terrible mistake in sleeping with DeMarcus. It seems like that is all he wanted to do since their first time. He was so rough where Jasper was so affectionate. Even worse, he had started to get possessive only days since when she first stayed the night.

She missed Jasper more than ever at that moment. He would have never acted like that towards her. She saw Tina on campus the week prior and a part of her wanted to confront her on messing up the time that she had with Jasper. It should have been her with the marriage proposal not that *stuck up bitch*. Her thoughts flashed back to how she practically begged for Jasper to not go back to Tina. The rumors about what transpired with Tim, Tina, and he had already started to get worse. Some said that Tim wanted revenge, some said that Tim and Tina were dating, and some said that Jasper almost went to jail for assault. Regardless of what happened, she wanted to reach out to him, but she stopped each time. Her phone never received a phone call from him, and that saddened her. She would have never slept with DeMarcus if she only got a call from the one she wanted.

She continued to stare at the phone regretting that she never picked it up days, even weeks prior. Her alarm on the phone rang to announce that her little break was over and that it was time to get dressed for class. Thirty seconds after that, DeMarcus texted her. She cringed as she read, *Hey baby. I know that you are about to go to class. Call me when you get out.*

Later that night, Shelia came to Jasper's room to give him more of her "candy". As much as Jasper enjoyed it, he was not impressed with her aggressiveness. She was so domineering and forceful, but being inside of her made him feel so superior at the same time. It was like she was putting on a show or something mainly for her amusement while she satisfied him. She gave him a workout each and every round. One to stay up on his fitness, he was able to keep up. That was a turn on for her.

They were in the midst of the act that night when one of the other InfoTech attendees stopped by to ask Jasper to join him for a drink. When he knocked on the door, he heard some rustling and almost walked away. He thought he heard some whispering and more rustling as he knocked again. Inside, Shelia was rushing into the bathroom as Jasper was rushing to throw on some clothes. When Jasper finally opened the door, his heart was beating hard as he thought that he was caught and couldn't get it together. Meanwhile, Shelia was standing in the shower butt naked while her clothes were stuffed under the bed in the room just as nervous, if not more.

Jasper thought quickly about how he would explain opening up the door with an erection under his shorts. He simply said, "Wow, you caught me....I was...ummm.... you know...ummm...talking to my girlfriend and just ummm...."

Shelia almost laughed out loud as the guy at the door replied with, "Whoa bro!! It's ok, man. I was going to get a drink at the bar, and I stopped to see if you were busy. I see that you are. I will see you later. Whoa!"

The two lustful coworkers sat on the bed after the interruption for a few minutes, giving time for the unwanted guest time to move away. Once their heartbeats slowed down, they quickly sped them back up as they resumed enjoying each other until they both had enough. It was going to be their last time getting it on during the conference, and they both took the action up a notch to enjoy it to the fullest. They eventually tired each other out and silently called a truce.

Leaving the next day going back to Memphis, Shelia had to make sure that her bedroom workout buddy would leave their experiences where they were. The ridicule and unprofessionalism had the potential to ruin her career. As good as it was to her, no dick was worth ruining all that she had worked for. She actually wanted her secret relationship to continue with Jasper from time to time, but she had to see where his head was. She thought that age would be a deterrent, and the last thing that she needed was a young, pussy-whipped guy parading around her office. As they laid there in his hotel bed, she rubbed his chest and asked, "So, we can keep this quiet, right? Keep it between us, and I will let the little boy get some candy from time to time." Jasper's eyes got big. "Jasper, what you think? You think you can keep it together?"

It was funny that the subject came up when it did because Jasper was thinking similar thoughts. He assumed mostly what she was thinking, but he thought about Rick's suspicions and worried about what he would do if any of it was substantiated. When Shelia stopped speaking, he jumped up to put on his underwear. Shelia underestimated him, and he felt compelled to put her in a proper boundary. He remembered his dad saying to a family friend years prior, "You see…when a man and woman are lying down together, they are on the same damn level then. No one is more powerful when you are both butt ass naked."

He looked back at the stunning, sweaty woman still waiting on an answer. She perked her eyebrows as if saying *I'm waiting.* At that point, Jasper's tendency to be a little too blunt kicked in without warning. As he inhaled his next breath, he spun around, looked at the beautiful body calling him, and said, "You must be used to weak lil dudes who fall for your intimidating, power play bullshit." He felt that she thought that it was some type of a treat for him to get a piece of her from time to time. She may have been the oldest in age, but he had experienced plenty of women like her. He also was not in a sexual drought.

He and various friends often talked over the years about the insecurities of women and the drama that arose because of it. Jasper always had an attraction to older women, and he realized through his attraction that some older women are just older girls in some ways. In seeing this, he saw that the insecurities that were there in younger age usually grew up as well with new logic and new manifesting problems stemming from the original causes.

These problems usually left the men that dealt with them few options on how to handle them.

For example, the need to look pretty is something that perhaps every young girl has come to deal with. It is possible that the same need transforms into various ways to validate acceptance and beauty as maturity transpires through the purchase of expensive purses or frolicking with men that make them feel pretty. The initial need is still there, but a host of other issues branch off from that need. Also, issues sometimes occur from the validation methods as well.

The same could be seen in Shelia. As beautiful and powerful of a woman she was, the scared little girl was visible in her that was probably crushed by rejection. Her life events seemingly had both positive and negative effects. That fear of rejection gave birth to the ambition and tenacity she exhibited, It propelled her into her career, but that same fear lead to many lonely nights without a suitor capable of loving her the way she wanted or the settling for knuckleheads that could only scratch the itch, physical or emotionally, but only for so long.

Shelia's looked changed to one of *Excuse you?* Undaunted, he continued his spill, "Wassup with the "come here lil boy" stuff? I hope that my words do not affect my job, but I don't like feeling like I am fucking my auntie." Realizing that he might have overdone it, he softened his gaze and his words.

"Check this out, Shelia.... I...ummm...like being with you. We can have fun together and both keep it quiet and both keep our jobs." He stressed the word both each time.

Shelia sat up, still stuck on the "fucking my auntie" part, she literally bit her lip. She was so used to power playing that she was dumbstruck when she was called out on it. She was seldom challenged in any way. She hesitated in her response. She wanted to curse him out, yet keep the avenue open to get some outstanding sex periodically. "Ok, Jasper. So, you feel like your fucking your auntie? Ok. Listen, I just had to ask if you were going to keep it quiet. That's all. You know how your boss Rick is looking for anything to get us on."

Jasper sat down next to Shelia and kissed her shoulder. He simply said, "Ok." He slid in the covers and pinched her on the ass, one cheek at a time.

Shelia laughed, "So I guess we are good. One thing though.....call me an auntie one more fucking time and I will crush your fucking nuts!" Jasper laughed and pinched her again. For an hour or so, they laid there talking about sex, their jobs, and Rick. She discussed what transpired afterwards on the day she broke up their talk in the hallway. It was quite apparent that Rick had to be dealt with carefully if they were going to continue hanging out after work hours.

Chapter 17

Saturday afternoon, Jasper returned from his trip looking forward to dozing off on his couch. After a couple of layovers, the InfoTech Solutions crew parted ways. He enjoyed learning a lot. He enjoyed leaving Memphis for a while. He enjoyed parlaying with Shelia.

He stopped by his parents' house first to grab some lunch and catch his parents up on the trip. They were excited for their son as his enthusiasm spewed in his descriptions and technical jargon that they didn't understand. They timidly brought up Tina in hopes to get an update as to what was going on without dampening his mood. When he heard the name, he frowned and politely changed the subject. They got the point and respected his need to heal on his own.

When his mom went upstairs to get the mail that he had forwarded to their house, Jasper tapped his dad on the shoulder and brought up Shelia. He whispered about how tired he was from getting it on with "an older chick". He was attempting to show his dad that he was ok after his heartbreak from Tina. His dad was extremely concerned and even contemplated calling her dad to discuss how down Jasper was. Jasper's attempt failed and spurred one of those "father-son-let's-go-outside-and-have-a-beer" moments.

"Boy, I felt the pain that you were going through in my soul. That type of pain doesn't just ease up with a couple pieces of pussy." Jasper learned that it is easier to just let his dad talk during these moments, and it was not to be repeated to his mom. That round of advice would be worse. "Jasper, just be careful out there. I know you all grown and shit, but let me tell you something. The best piece of pussy I ever had....is pussy that I never had." He heard that last portion from his father an uncountable amount of times. He was basically saying that one should be careful and not get caught up. His dad's old school logic was that a woman can be the best and the worst thing to ever happen to a man...period.

By the time Jasper returned to his apartment, he was fatigued more than expected. He threw his suitcase in the room, used the bathroom, and sat on his couch to watch some TV. He made a sandwich for dinner before passing out. While he was reaching for a plate in his cabinet, he noticed that there was a glass on the counter that he didn't remember using prior to leaving. Tina favored that glass when she stayed there. Without thinking too much about it, Jasper placed it in the sink.

The next evening, Sonya was on her way over to Jasper's place to hang out. She listened to Rodney's advice and humbly initiated the conversation to be in Jasper's presence again. Of course, Jasper welcomed the chance to kick it with the beautiful songstress. She was fun to be with and eager to please without any hesitation. After dealing with Shelia, he was ready to just enjoy himself and not feel the pressure of not being good enough or stress from her supervisory status.

Around 7 p.m., the soft spoken beauty walked in and greeted him with a big hug. After a lot of thought, she decided to just let things happen with Jasper. She held no expectations and was ready for either bliss or disappointment. Life had recently dealt her a series of emotional blows, and she just wanted to feel better. She hoped that being with Jasper would help her relax.

Small talked lasted only moments before lights were being turned off and clothes started getting tossed on the floor. Jasper gave her the relaxation that she needed and wanted. She was so relaxed that she felt comfortable staying the night, whereas leaving was always her control mechanism. Comfortable and bold, she rolled over to face him and bluntly asked, "I know you have to work in the morning, but you mind if I lie next to you tonight?"

As Rodney knew, Jasper was not too happy about how she left the last time that they tussled in the sheets. He stifled a smile and proceeded to push the envelope that she just placed herself in. "Oh, so noooow you wanna stay the night. I almost dozed off, but I had to be ready to come lock the door behind you when you left."

She looked at him in shock, but understood that it was payback for how she did him earlier. She dejectedly got up and proceeded to get dressed. As she found her bra, she stated, "Ok. I guess that I deserve that. Ok, buddy, you got me back." Jasper's eyes were telling Sonya even more just then. That behind the macho act that just occurred, he was hurting more than ever. Instead of leaving, she quipped back with "Well, now that we are even….since you got me back….let's call it a draw. To celebrate this draw, how about you give me some more of that sweet dick, and I hook you up with some sweet breakfast before you roll to the office. Deal?" Jasper only smiled and pulled back the covers beckoning her to come back. "Go ahead and take you a nap, so you can give me some more of that long stroke."

Usually when there is something secretly going on between a man and a woman, it is said others can usually tell by watching the woman. The overcompensating attempts to hide the reality or the not-so-subtle acts of jealousy and protecting one's interest are so obvious to those who actually pay attention.

Sometimes the male is the telltale, but Shelia proved the saying true in the next weeks after the conference. Jasper was able to play it cool at all times, and both were able to play it cool around Rick at all times. It was the not-so-subtle acts of jealousy on her part that raised questions to some of the ladies that worked in the walls of InfoTech Solutions.

Jasper had felt the fresh meat syndrome when he first started with the company. Various lunch invitations, trouble tickets that requested him specifically, and the occasional bold conversation in one of the break rooms were some of the ways that he was informed of what some of the women thought about him. It calmed down a little once word got out that he had a girlfriend. It picked back up suddenly, and Jasper was curious as to why. A fast talking, self-titled "professional cougar and biker chick" gave him the insight that he wanted. She was a project assurance specialist and known to be a flirt as well.

He was attempting to diagnose an issue that the biker chick, Paula Christie Demming, was having with installing some new software. While he was typing some commands into the keyboard, she tapped him on the shoulder and said to him, "Eww chile, I have never seen Ms. Bunton walk down this aisle so much in a couple years. Those eyes undressed you, licked your ear, and rode you until the sun set in the west!"

Jasper's heart jumped when he heard Shelia's last name, but he didn't look away from the screen. "What did you say, Ms. Demming?" He had seen Shelia walk past the area once, but he thought nothing of it.

Paula went into her infamous laugh that would make anyone smile regardless of how bad a day was going for them. She leaned in a little closer and said, "Mr. Hooks, a gal like me has loved a many and left a many alone. I know what I am talking about. If you want a piece of that, it may be yours for the taking. I'm just saying chile!"

Jasper just replied with, "Umm ok, Ms. Demming." He wasn't going to let on that he already had a piece of Shelia.

Minutes later, Shelia walked by again. This time, Ms. Demming stopped her. "Hey girl." The two women chatted for a few minutes while Jasper continued to resolving the discovered issue. He intentionally made no eye contact, but he did watch her mannerisms out of the corner of his eye. When she left, the observant cougar leaned in again and said to him. "I told you." She was right, but Jasper wasn't going to let her know that she was right. "Honey, you didn't seem too interested in her though. Maybe you like a different type of woman." He felt even more uneasy as Paula made a weak attempt with that last statement to put herself in the prospect pool of Jasper's admirers.

Jasper struggled to keep his professionalism at that point. He stopped himself from making a quirky remark back just to be flirtatious in return. He looked at Paula and thought that she didn't look too bad. He wasn't into blondes at all plus it seemed that years of motorcycle riding gave her a rough, tanned look that wasn't appealing to him. He imagined that it would be kind of fun to flirt back, but he didn't want her to get the wrong idea. Also, he didn't want Sheila to get the wrong idea in case she was still snooping around trying to look busy.

In the following days, Jasper silently watched Shelia, her interactions with him, and how other females interacted with him when she was around. He thought that maybe he was imagining what would seem obvious to the more nosey employees who knew them, but no one said anything directly to him. He was happy that no one did.

It had been a couple of days since DeMarcus had heard from Tara. He was kicking himself for being so harsh to her the last time that they spoke. He didn't mean to call her a bitch. He didn't mean to tell her that she could be replaced. In their heated conversation, she brought up an old story about something that she used to do with Jasper. At that point, the conversation went from seductive to both sides spitting fiery words at each other. Nasty things were said, and the possibility of something magical fizzled out before it could truly begin. That is how DeMarcus saw it anyway.

He sat on the couch where he first kissed Tara and wondered if she would ever answer his call. It was obvious that she was not over Jasper, and it angered him. Once before, he fell for a girl that seemed to worship Jasper just like Tara. Sadly, she didn't give DeMarcus the time of day because she only had eyes for Jasper. Sad for her, Jasper was seeing Tara and didn't even notice how deep that the girl had feelings for him. Jasper had left Tara for Tina, and his frat brother Tim had recently told him how things went down outside of the Memphis apartment. The circle of unrequited affection started back where it began and no one was with anyone.

Anger seethed through the misguided and lonely guy on the couch. He wasn't sure if he was more mad at himself or Tara for saying that she didn't want to see his "crazy, punk ass again." The one thing that he was sure of was that Jasper had affected his happiness again. That is how DeMarcus saw it anyway, and for that realization he was furious.

Chapter 18

It was preferred that Jasper come to Shelia's loft townhouse in Germantown when they got together for their weekly rendezvous. He had to be convinced to stop by that night after the two secret lovers had a talk about her suspicious behavior around InfoTech Solutions. Some say that when one person in a non-platonic relationship gets too attached it is often called catching feelings. Jasper suspected that Shelia had indeed caught some feelings after they had been dealing with each other for a little while. The arrangement, which was just occasional sex from time to time, was almost defunct because of that fact.

Nonetheless, he found himself showering and heading to her place. What started off as sex with a powerful seductress slowly meshed into something sprinkled with passion and laced with long talks and laughter afterwards. Jasper liked her and enjoyed being with her, but they both knew that the relationship would never blossom into anything more. It wasn't necessarily the difference in age or her supervisory status. Deep down, they knew that the other had other things going on. Deep down, they both knew that the train was going to only make so many stops. Until then, they were going to enjoy the ride.

The night began the same way it always did when he went over there. They talked, had a couple of drinks, clothes dropped, sex happened, and they talked while they waited until the next round. Their dialogue that night was slightly off. It was as if Shelia wanted to say something more than what she was discussing.

"Ummm, I love it when you come through." She kissed him on the forehead and got up to get some water. When she returned, Jasper was staring at her as if he was trying to dissect her thoughts. She saw the look in his eyes and said, "What's wrong with you, lover? Why are you looking at me like that?"

Jasper tried to metaphorically bite his tongue, but he had to get his thoughts off of his chest. "Boo, what's wrong with you? Something is weird, but I don't know what." They sat in the bed embraced like they had been lovers for years. Shelia's dark skin seemed to give off the perfect luster glowing in the light of the candles burning in various spots in the bedroom. She remained silent and only regarded him with her troubled eyes.

She finally spoke after a long sigh and replied with a question, "Is everything ok with you? I mean, is everything really ok with you?" There was actual concern in her eyes when she finally looked him back in the eyes. The mood for additional play was broken by the solemn shift in conversation. Whatever she was thinking was not going to come out of her mouth. Jasper thought that their conversation about her office antics was about to come back up, but she changed the subject. "Let's just enjoy right now. Ok?"

He leaned back on the pillows, closed his eyes, and took in the scent of her perfume. "Ok." He knew that the talk would be continued later. Before he had to drive home, he wanted to just feel her body next to his with minimal drama. Whatever she wanted to say would have to wait for he was not in the mood to really hear it. For a few more hours they laid mostly in silence with some part of their bodies touching, enjoying each other's presence.

Vivian decided to call the number that was given to her by a friend a second time. The first time, the generic voicemail instantly sounded with its default "please leave a message" speech. She hung up and decided to not leave a message. This time, a tired voice answered, "Hello?"

Vivian was ecstatic, yet nervous. "Hey Jasper. This is Vivian. Ray gave me your number and said that you moved back to Memphis after graduation. I was asking him to show me around the next time that I came to town, but he doesn't live there anymore. He gave me your number instead."

It took him a minute to realize who he was talking to, and he was focusing on driving back home after leaving Shelia's place. He halfway heard what she said. "Hey Vivian! What's going on? What made Ray give you my number?" He was in the marching band with Ray while he was at Pembrook, but he didn't know him that well. He wondered how Ray got the number to even give to her. He remembered the over 6-foot-tall Vivian and knew that she was in the same sorority as Tina. He had seen her at some of the parties and occasionally on campus. She had graduated the year before him.

"Well, I will be in town next week for a business meeting. If you got time can you be like…my tour guide….and show me a couple of places to eat and hang out?" Jasper saw no threat in the request. He joked back, "Sure. I can like….show you a couple of spots. Call me when you make it to town, and tell Ray I said, "Hey." They talked for a couple of minutes until Jasper pulled up to his apartment. He ended the conversation and yawned. He was wondering why she would need a tour guide around Memphis since she used to go to Pembrook. Almost everyone who was a student there hung out in Memphis; it was just that close.

Vivian smiled a scheming smile as she hung up. She was about to try to get some of what her sorority sister told her so much about. She called her cousin to verify that she would indeed come to Memphis to visit, and she laid out the plan in case she needed somewhere to stay even though she was hoping that she wouldn't need to. Jasper's bedroom was the goal of this trip, and she was gearing up for the challenge.

Unbeknownst to Jasper or Vivian, Tina was planning a trip to Memphis that weekend as well. She added a couple of items to the bag that she kept in the car containing various things that she wanted to use with Jasper to rekindle their relationship. It contained an apologetic card, condoms, and a bottle of his favorite vodka among other things. She had a few more things to pick up but decided to do so after she left work later that night.

She was hopeful that all would go as planned. She discussed how she would execute her plan with her mother again and took mental notes during their conversation. The bonding of mother and daughter again warmed Tina's heart, though it was under some bizarre circumstances. What truly made her heart flutter was that she would soon be in the presence of Jasper again. This time she planned on doing it right and never leaving his presence, mind, or heart again.

There is a phrase commonly used that says that one's ears are burning when someone is talking about them. If there was absolute truth to that, Jasper's ears would have been undeniably sizzling that night. Shelia was talking to one of her best friends in New York about the young thing that just left her place while Vivian was talking to her cousin and making travel plans. Tina was talking to her mother while Kyle and Rodney were discussing how their old roommate was doing. Jasper's parents were preparing for bed and were discussing a phone call that came from Tina's dad earlier. Added to the list of people talking about Jasper were a couple of his other frat brothers.

Earlier that day, Tim and DeMarcus hooked up to grab something to eat. Actually, DeMarcus was snooping to see what happened in Memphis with Tina at Jasper's place. Subconsciously, he also wanted to vent to someone that may feel similar to what he felt about their popular frat brother. The conversation made them both laugh at how they had sex with ladies that Jasper had adored and renewed anger on how their respective situations panned out.

They decided to get together and talk more at DeMarcus's apartment later than evening. While the subject of Jasper was popular that night, DeMarcus was texting Tara when Tim showed up. Tara didn't respond to any of his texts until he typed, "I bet that you still in love with your boy Jasper. Fuck that dude."

Infuriated, Tara broke her digital silence and texted back, "You wish you were him." That would be the first and last text that she would send him. The rage that swept over DeMarcus seeded the conversation he had with Tim.

It was obvious that Tim had liked Tina just as DeMarcus liked Tara. They talked about how they felt, how sex was with the two ladies, and how Jasper didn't appreciate them. The rumor was true that Tim wanted revenge due to what happened outside of Jasper's apartment. DeMarcus joked, "Frat, you did fuck his fiancé. I would've fucked you up too." The joke was not well received at all. It was almost scary how Tim reacted as he sat looking at the ceiling making a growling sound for almost a minute. "Damn bruh! My bad....it was just a joke."

Chapter 19

The following Thursday morning Vivian picked up a rental car and headed to Memphis. To furnish the fallacy that she was actually on a business trip instead of one of a personal nature, she thought that it was a minor expense. She grabbed a briefcase, threw some papers in there for noise and effect, and threw it on the front seat. She gathered a couple of outfits and other gear, then she headed towards Memphis. She planned in her mind how she would entice Jasper into satisfying her curiosity. If it didn't work out, she already planned to have a fun weekend with her cousin as a consolation prize.

Jasper, on the other hand, started his day as he normally would. He woke up in his apartment, did a little workout, grabbed some fruit and a Pop Tart, and headed to work. He spoke to Vivian the night before to confirm that they would meet for lunch. She stated that she would have a break in dealing with clients, etc. for most of Thursday and wanted to meet up. She wanted barbeque, so he suggested Interstate BBQ.

Jasper was able to head to lunch a little early in an attempt to beat the lunch crowd. He asked Vivian to meet him at the restaurant around 10:45. She smiled as she agreed on the phone. The recollection of the graphic account from Tina of how he performed during sex excited her and pushed out any thoughts of how trifling the trip was. She thought to herself, *Tina shouldn't have let him go like that. She knows that good dick is hard to find.*

They hugged as they met in front of the restaurant and took a seat inside after ordering their meals. Jasper was oblivious to Vivian's true intent, since he assumed that Tina and Vivian were close. He first thought that the lunch was set up by Tina and had sent Vivian in to be a negotiator so that he gave the relationship another chance. Tina's text messages had trickled to only one a day. Jasper was guarded and ready to deflect any mention of Tina by Vivian. He wasn't prepared for what Vivian was really going to say.

She sliced the silence with small talk about the clients she had to see and talk about her cousin. She discussed attending Pembrook's homecoming festivities and asked him if he was going. The mention of homecoming cracked the defensive wall Jasper had placed around him. He excitedly talked about playing cymbals in the alumni band and how the parties would be. Vivian, as if she sensed those cracks, threw in a quick comment to test the waters.

"So, do you think that things would be weird if you ran into Tina during homecoming?" Jasper momentarily stopped chewing his sandwich. "I'm sorry, Jasper. I kinda heard what happened, and I shouldn't have brought it up." Jasper braced himself for comments like, *You should give her a call* or *She misses you.* What came out of Vivian's mouth instead was, "I love my sister and all, but she messed up. Good guys like you don't come around all of the time. I am sorry that she did you like that, and I hope that you don't be bitter. I apologize for bringing it up. Let's just enjoy lunch."

Jasper resumed chewing not sure what to say in response. He couldn't decide whether he was really being set up by Tina or if she was being sincere. Vivian sat there thinking that no response was a good response, so she continued to press on with her scheme. Minutes after some more small talk, she interjected another Tina-themed conversation point that was probing, yet flirtatious. "It is so nice seeing you again, and I just have to thank you so much for taking time during lunch to hang out with me. I won't tell Tina that we hung out. If she knew better, she would be here now."

Jasper unfazed any longer by Tina's name decided to ask, "She sent you here, huh?" He noticed the shift in her sitting and the way she was eating, which became overly suggestive as the lunch went on. He had to return to work soon, so he wanted to feed his curiosity to why she was there, like he was feeding his craving for barbeque. Vivian was truly taken aback by his question, and he pushed on. "I mean….I know you came here for work, but you sure that y'all didn't talk about trying to get us back together? That ain't happening, so…"

She chose to cut off his next statement with a whistle and retorted, "Boo boo, you and I eating lunch here ain't got nothing to do with her. I didn't get the pleasure of getting to know you that much before I left Pembrook, and Ray gave me your number because he said that you know the best spots in Memphis. If I wanted something else, I wouldn't go through this much trouble."

Her tall frame intimidated many guys during her time at Pembrook. She was the same height as Jasper, 6 feet, 2 inches. Needless to say, he wasn't intimidated at all, and he thought that her little speech was cute with the attitude mannerisms and all. "Alright, I got ya. I hear ya." She sat back in her chair and continued with her inquisitive flirting. Jasper started to verify that there was some attraction to him by her. He knew it the moment they saw each other in the parking lot of the restaurant. If she was truly there for business and just called him to have fun, he was going to see for sure.

As the talk moved on, she stated that she would be done for the day around 6 p.m. "Jasper, thanks for meeting me for lunch. The barbeque was good, but the company was better. I see that you are pretty cool. Let's hang out again for dinner....my treat." Jasper saw that she couldn't look him in the eye and figured that those words signified her attempt to play her hand. He really wasn't in the mood to deal with anymore females. Shelia and Sonya kept him satisfied and aggravated at the same time. His curiosity was tickled by Vivian though. She was known around the schoolyard back in the day for being aggressive and having pretty nipples to some of the guys that experienced her and told about it.

He played it cool and replied, "I got some things to do when I get off, but I should be done around 7:30." He still felt that he was being set up by Tina, but he was not going to worry about it. If Tina had the audacity to show up, then he felt that she could take the cursing out that he would unleash on her and Vivian. If he was wrong, he would at least get a free meal if nothing else.

Vivian was entirely too obvious in her attempt to play it cool as she replied back with, "Ok. I am looking forward to having an even better time with you later. I will call you around 7 to see what's up."

After a quick hug, they parted ways. Jasper continued his day at work and rushed home to clean up his apartment, just in case dinner with Vivian ended there. He texted Kyle with a quick summary of the lunch meeting. He hollered before he responded with, "Really? Pretty Titty Vivian? Aw hell naw!"

Vivian went shopping and stopped by her cousin's house to take a nap. The way that Tina described Jasper, she would need the rest.

Tina was on her way to Memphis with the intent on setting up her surprise in Jasper's apartment before he returned home from work. She prayed before she got on the road that everything would go well. She envisioned how she would light the candles and dance around the apartment as she changed clothes. She saw herself hugging him as he started to cuss and fuss, silencing his rage. She saw herself squeezing the fight out of him as he realized that he missed her and that she was really sorry. Her daydreams always ended with intense makeup sex and a renewed relationship.

She arrived around 4 p.m. which gave her an hour and a half to set up before he got home. She sat in the car and played with the key that she schemed to get for a few minutes. Each time she reached to open the door, she stopped. Doubt had started to set in and flooded her mind. *What if he got mad and kicked me out? Called the cops? He never accepted any of my calls or answered any of my texts. What if I see another bitch's stuff up in there?* She felt herself getting sick and almost started crying.

She drove all that way and couldn't even get out of the car. She recalled how Tim was looking while lying down and begging Jasper to stop hitting him. She felt lightheaded as she kept trying to get her hand to open up her door to step out. All of the planning to get to that point was about to be ruined if she stayed there. "God, please give me the strength to do this…to make this right," was whispered in a crackly voice.

Twenty minutes went by, and she still sat there frozen in her thoughts and paralyzed by her doubt. The clock on her car stereo displayed 4:52. Jasper was due to get off work any minute and was going to be on his way home. She felt desperate as she finally opened up her car door and stepped out. She was wobbly as she retrieved her bag out of the trunk and made her way up the stairs to where he stayed. She held the key in her hand with tears in her eyes. Her dreams never included rejection, and the possibility of rejection was stifling her desire to enter the domain where she was once happy, with a man that adored her.

Dejected, she crumbled under the pressure and ran back to her car. She slung the bag she carried in her backseat. She screamed and rocked as she banged on her steering wheel. "I can't do it! I can't do it!" Minutes before the person she wanted to see was set to arrive, she started her car and drove to the other side of the apartment complex. She needed time to get herself together.

She cursed, cried, and talked to herself until she was calm enough to head back to the city of Pembrook.

Vivian called as promised, and Jasper was ready for her. They both stated that they had to work the following day so their plans could not last all night or involve heavy partying. Jasper fought the urge to offer for her to just come over; it was too forward and didn't involve dinner. They settled on a seafood restaurant on Beale Street that he used to go to and agreed to meet at 8:15. Vivian had figured that she would go in for the kill during dinner or just enjoy it while setting up for a future time.

They arrived and embraced each other just as friendly as they did earlier. They proceeded to walk inside, and Jasper purposely walked behind her in order to get a good look. She was very hippy for her height but lacked a large posterior. Regardless, he was more excited about seeing her bare chest. Vivian, on the other hand, wanted to get the workout that Tina told her she used to get. When she parked, she thought about something Tina said, "Girl, he had me passed out after we would get down. He used to wear me out." She was hoping for the same effect later.

The conversation started light as they waited for their meals to arrive. She ordered a pasta dish with crab and scallops, and Jasper decided to try the sampler called the Pirate Platter. As they started eating, Vivian started coming on stronger with the hints that she was dropping. "I wish that I would've hung out with you more in undergrad. You are such a sweetie." More comments followed with an occasional lick of the lips or seductive eye glance.

Jasper had decided that Tina was not involved at all and allowed his silver tongue to speak words to see where the evening could head. Vivian, getting blunter as the dinner continued, dropped the comment, "If it wasn't for Tina, I would have to see what you are really about. I hope that doesn't scare you." Jasper took that as his cue to seal the deal and offered a trip to his place to talk more. Vivian smiled as she said, "Sure." Minutes later, the waiter brought the check and asked if they wanted any dessert. Vivian chuckled and said back to him, "I think we don't need any more calories to burn later." She paid for the meal, and they proceeded to head to his place.

They were going at it in no time after walking in the door to his apartment. They kissed passionately (just as Tina said that he always did). He took off his shirt before reaching for her clothes (just as Tina said that he always did). A few more minutes of touching and fondling ensued before Jasper rushed to unhook her bra. He received the prize he waited for and saw what he had heard so much about. To him, her breasts were indeed flawless and golden like freshly baked biscuits with areolas looking like the biscuits had been dipped in honey. He smirked as he could now add his name to the list of those who had the privilege of seeing why she was known as, "Pretty Titty" Vivian.

She smirked back with the assurance that she was about to experience what she had desired ever since that lunch in Pembrook. Any loyalty to her sorority sister was nonexistent as her flesh answered only to her own self-seeking yearnings. Neither one of them thought about Tina and would never tell her.

Around 1 a.m., Vivian was awakened softly for a quick second round before the rendezvous was to end. He massaged each breast with appreciation for their loveliness. She rubbed his back and chest with gratitude and vigor before he opened her long light-skinned legs to enter her. Jasper had been in situations like this before, where both parties enjoyed the moment without plans of hearing from each other anytime soon. They both knew that the option to rumble would be open whenever their paths crossed again. Her anticipation added to her climax, each one of them. His eyes were closed as her breathing sped up. When he opened them, the sight of her breasts sped up his time before ejaculation.

Before he was ready, he came and ended the second round with Vivian. They were both satisfied and tired. Without speaking, Vivian got up to get dressed in the bathroom. Once she stepped out, she mumbled something about having to see an important client in only a few hours and headed toward the door. Jasper walked her to the door and convinced her to show her breasts to him one more time. They both laughed as she did what he requested. As she pulled her shirt back down and fixed her bra, she walked out the door.

He felt kind of dirty after Vivian left. Tina knew Vivian, but Vivian came on to him. It was that reality which allowed him to go back to sleep, without any regrets for his actions. Before he dozed off though, his mind twirled with flashbacks of his sex life over the last couple of weeks. He had been with Shelia, Sonya, and Vivian all in less than a week and a half. He also had new offers from Ashante at work and a girl he met at a grocery store. He knew that his sexual appetite was only temporarily fulfilling the craving for love that he once felt. Eventually he drifted off to sleep. He had a long day coming at work in merely hours, and little did he know, his weekend was about to be even longer.

Earlier, while Jasper and Vivian were fulfilling their individual objectives in his apartment, a black car drove by four times. Each time, the driver took mental notes of the surroundings and moved on. One of those times, the driver pulled into one of the parking spots and made a couple of phone calls before moving on.

Tina hoped that Jasper would go to church with his mom as he sometimes did on Sundays. She happened to be right, but stayed in the car for a while before finally going up to the apartment. She'd made the drive from Pembrook again and wasn't going back until she saw him. She went back and forth about whether or not she would go through with it the entire weekend. Ms. Jackson convinced her to, "pursue what you want and make him want you again."

She briskly walked up the stairs to the second floor, opened the door with the key that she was given, and slammed it once she was inside. She moved quickly to minimize disbelief among any neighbors that may have seen her, as well as to keep herself from turning back around. She felt dizzy as she leaned against the closed door, and she contemplated the legalities of her actions, and the unpredictability of Jasper.

The place was very disheveled, but she didn't have long before the timeframe in which he would typically get back. She prayed silently and got started with the setup. She washed the dishes in the sink and wiped the tables and counters. She replaced the sheets on the bed with a red satin sheet set that she had ordered and she sprinkled fake rose petals on the bed and carpet in the bedroom. She placed new candles around the apartment and a bottle of champagne and two glasses in the freezer like Jasper used to do for her. She finished her set up by setting a bowl of strawberries and a bowl of chocolate on the coffee table with various sauces and creams.

Satisfied, she went to use the bathroom and get ready. She looked under the sink and in the trash can for anything that she would find suspicious. She didn't find anything and smiled as she tried to put everything back as she found it. She glanced at her watch and rushed to get in place. She prayed again asking God for strength to get through the evening and for a chance to make things right with Jasper.

Minutes later, she sat on the couch watching TV at a low volume, constantly listening for any noise to signify that Jasper was coming up the stairs. Her nervousness made her hands sweat and her mouth dry. She grabbed a glass from the cupboard and drank two glasses of tap water. She tensely checked all the candles to ensure that they were lit. She watched the time and played with the arrangement of rose petals on the bed. She paced and sprayed on more perfume.

Sometime around 5 p.m., she was close to dozing off when she heard the rustle of keys. She jumped up and posed on the edge of the couch and pushed the play button on the remote control that managed Jasper's stereo. She felt her heartbeat race as he entered and looked her in the eyes. He dropped what was in his hands and drew back a defensive fist in response.

"What the fuck?" The entry door was still open as Jasper stood there with his heart beating fast and trying to conceive what was actually happening. "What….wh …what…the hell are you doing here? How the fuck did you get in here?" Tina didn't budge, giving Jasper time to calm down. She wanted to approach him and kiss him badly, but the cursing was an indication that all was not as perfect, as she wanted it to be. She wasn't going to give up that easily. She had come too far.

"So, you just going to stand there and not say anything? You got two minutes to say something before I call the cops. How did you get a key? Gimme my damn key back. What the fuck is wrong with you?" Jasper continued his rant for a couple of minutes as he picked up his stuff and closed the door. He noticed the candles and peeked into his bedroom to see the setup. Anger swelled up more and more inside of him as tears began to well up in the corners of Tina's eyes. "Answer me and get the fuck out of here!"

Tina, frightened at first, suddenly felt a wave of calm and leaned into Jasper for a kiss. He simply sidestepped her, grabbed her forearms and spun her around. He almost started crying as his anger was starting to intertwine with the recollection of what happened in his bedroom months prior and all that he had endured since. "Hey baby…I am soooo…sorry. I want to show you that I messed up and want to do better. Just give me a chance." The tears broke their temporary sanctuary in Tina's eyes and smeared the makeup on her face as she pleaded sincerely.

Jasper looked at her ass in the outfit she was wearing and was instantly aroused. The thought of rubbing it and spreading her cheeks fleeted just as fast as it came in. He wanted her to leave, but she had to answer a few questions first. "Fuck you Tina! You think that you can just break into my apartment, get all naked, and I will just take you back?"

Tina persisted and grabbed at him as he moved around to avoid her. She was pleading desperately as he inquired. Finally, she fell to her knees and started crying uncontrollably.

Jasper felt sorry for her for a moment. Looking at her on her knees was not an attractive look for someone that he once loved. Deep down, he still felt something for her. Some say that hatred is a function of love, and the balance of love versus hate was leaning not so much in Tina's favor. He swallowed the urge to say, "Get the fuck up, and get the fuck out of here" so he could get the answers he felt he deserved. She slowly rose and mumbled, "I love you baby…I…freaking love you." She faced him and saw him casually snacking on the fruit that was on his coffee table. She saw her opportunity fading….and fading fast. If he wanted to talk, she was going to talk.

It was definitely obvious then that the episode with Vivian had nothing to do with the current one. He felt relief in that and was actually thinking about calling her soon. He was so consumed in his thoughts that he didn't notice the anger in the face staring at him. When he caught her gaze, her countenance had changed back to one of sadness and desperation. He was larger and faster than her, but he kept his distance from her. Anyone who could cheat on him in his own bed, and manipulate their way into his apartment, was probably capable of anything. He didn't trust her.

Dejected, Tina looked out of the window at the sun that was almost gone down and welcoming the night. She had envisioned that she would be making love to her man by then, after saying a few words. He seemed callous and unforgiving standing there distant and continuing to snack on fruit. She felt happy to be so close to him and crestfallen in that she wasn't as close to him as she wanted. She wanted to hug him, but he would push her away again. His patience was fading with every second. He attested that fact when he snarled, "I'm waiting, Tina!"

She took a deep breath and quickly dropped her lingerie. Jasper was not expecting that and dropped the strawberry that he was eating. She tried to look sexy as she said, "Ok, baby. I will answer your questions.....all of them. First, I want you know how much I love your crazy ass." She was thinking about her mom as she walked over to the bag she brought with her and pulled out a bottle of baby oil. "I fucked up, Jasper. Damn, I fucked up!" She commenced to rubbing oil over her breasts first and then her thighs. Jasper's only movement was pivotal in that he wanted to face and watch her at all times. He was visibly excited and slightly scared. "Let's not talk about it right now though. I want you to take off your clothes and let me rub some of this oil on you."

Jasper stood by his coffee table silent, frozen in disbelief, not knowing what to do. Part of him wanted to let her words come to fruition, but he couldn't move. He jumped around in his thoughts. He went over the good times with Tina, the fight with Tim, the new women in his life, the lonely nights, etc. His thoughts shuffled and settled on the night that he left Tara to focus on his relationship with Tina. Finally, he started laughing loudly. Tina saw an opening and went in again for a kiss.

Jasper saw the oiled, nude body, out of the corner of his eye approach him, and he braced himself for the contact. He allowed the kiss and grabbed her ass harshly. Tina felt successful until he pushed her back and wiped his hands on his shirt. "Tina, your time is up. I gave you time to say anything to convince me that you deserved another chance. That was fucking weak. Muthafucka, that shit was weak!"

The tears returned, and Tina could only scream, "Please baby. Please!"

He thought about how Tara asked him not to go to Tina because she was "shady and crazy". He now agreed and was angry that he chose wrong. There was no way that Tara would take him back. He spat at Tina, "I sleep on the couch....a lot....because I can't stand to lay in this bed alone sometimes. I couldn't even trust my girl or my frat brothers. For you, I didn't have enough, and they wanted what I had."

She got close enough to kiss him again, and he dismissed her to keep talking. She grabbed for his penis, and he looked at her as if to say, *Are you serious?* "First, give me my key back. Then tell me something.... something."

The tears weren't getting her any sympathy, so she stopped crying. The sight of her naked body didn't spark passion, so she started looking for her clothes. Her pleading didn't give her a second chance, but she wasn't done asking yet. "Baby, I already said that I fucked up. I have fucking been dealing with that hurt, but I can't take it back. I want....I need....A second chance to show you that I am what you need."

Her words meant nothing to Jasper. He wanted to hear why she had sex with Tim, how many times it happened, and how did it all start. He wanted to hear why Tim of all people and why in his bed. Money was not a valid reason in his eyes, so she would have to do better than that. He knew she couldn't say anything valid, so his eyes regarded her oily body for what he knew was the last time, as he verbally slashed at her simply to vent the frustrations he never really got off of his chest.

Instead of admitting to their wrongdoings, some people only seek to blame you and your wrongdoings, in order to justify their actions. Instead of trying to be remorseful or sincerely sorry about their actions, they try to act disinterested or even bold. It is sadly common to hear phrases from guilty parties such as *You don't know how I feel right now*, or *I don't want to talk about that right now*. Then there are the statements that seem to displace ownership like, *I wouldn't have done it, if you were more...* During their exchange, Tina had made such statements. Jasper's thinking was saying as he listened, *What the fuck?!? Fuck how you feel, since you are the one that did wrong,* but the shock of what he was hearing left him speechless and sorry that he ever loved such a conniving woman.

The moon had already replaced the sun in the Memphis skyline, and the candles that Tina bought provided the only light inside of the small one bedroom apartment. They went back and forth talking at each other and not really listening to each other at all. Jasper was speaking his mind, while Tina screamed for forgiveness. After a while Jasper had enough and started asking her to leave. Tina wasn't done fighting yet, "Jasper, can we just do it one more time?" She waited for an answer and started rubbing her chest seductively.

He thought about it and considered roughly taking his annoyance out on her body as a cruel way to say his final goodbye. He decided against it because he didn't want her to think that there was a chance of patching things up or to experience any pleasure that he could give her. "No, you should leave now."

He blew out the candles that were still lit and hid one in his bathroom to use for future exploits. She started packing up what she wanted but left the candy, fruit, the sheets, as well as some of the other stuff. She madeit a point to grab the toys she bought and a handful of the fake rose petals. Jasper followed her around to keep her moving and turned on lights, but stayed a distance from her. No more words were spoken, and the level of tension rose rapidly. She hurriedly grabbed what she wanted before she felt too overwhelmed. She turned toward the one that she loved and said, "Can we just sit down and talk, Jasper? I mean, I…just…need you….to…"

Jasper just looked toward the door and dropped his head. Tina caught the hint and walked out, not looking back. Jasper rushed to the door to lock it and latch the chain. He made a mental note to request a lock change the next day. He sat back on the couch conflicted. He wanted to call her back and give her the chance to talk that she wanted, but his common sense told him that he did the right thing. He resumed eating the fruit that was left in the bowl and called Kyle. "Bruh, you ain't going believe what the fuck just happened."

While Tina was begging Jasper to lower his voice, the same black car from the previous Thursday made a couple of rounds past building J of the Evercrest Apartments. The driver recognized Tina's car parked in the distance on one of the rotations around and mumbled, "Ain't that bout a bitch!" For the past couple of weeks, the driver of the car drove through those apartments checking out Jasper's apartment and anything that stood out about the neighbors and the neighborhood. The phone sitting on the passenger seat rang as the car was leaving the complex. The driver answered and only said into the phone, "Yep", then hung up.

A couple of hours later, the driver noticed a sniveling Tina rushing to her car. She was observed sitting there for about 20 minutes before leaving. Shortly after, the driver left as well.

Chapter 20

Jasper found it hard to sleep and spent a lot of that night cleaning up all that Tina had set up in his apartment. He laughed to himself as he noticed a plant placed next to bed that he didn't see before. There was a card taped to it with a long note apologizing, begging for another chance, and explaining the purpose of the plant. The plant was meant to represent the *'growth of their love for each other* and that she would *water it daily as each day presents new opportunities for nourishment of that love.'* He knew instantly after reading it that Tina's mom had a say-so in the idea about the plant. He balled up the note and tossed it into the bathroom garbage can. He decided to keep the plant though. There was no need to throw a healthy plant away, and his apartment could use the decoration.

Exhausted from the ordeal earlier and the cleanup, he collapsed on his bed. After lying in the new sheets on his bed, he felt compelled to leave. He called Shelia, who invited him to spend the night at her place. They talked briefly when he got there and slept. The mood for intimacy was not present, and Jasper felt safer being away in case Tina had another key.

The next three days were uneventful for the most part. There were no phone calls or text messages from Tina, but Mr. Hooks called Tuesday to tell him that he heard from Tina's dad. He apologized for his daughter's and wife's actions after he heard about it. Rodney and Kyle called Jasper daily to check on him and offer their takes on the situation.

Thursday morning, Shelia sent Jasper a text message asking him to meet her in one of the smaller conference rooms that was seldom used. She checked out the key under the guise of *Policy Review Session* and waited until he arrived. Reluctantly, Jasper stopped by after completing a trouble ticket to see what the urgency was about. He knocked, entered the room and closed the door behind him. He made sure that no one was in the hallway when he entered. He saw Shelia, looking stunning and distraught, sitting amongst a stack of paperwork and white binders.

Shelia seemed to be in business mode and didn't look up at Jasper. She asked him to sit down, he did as she asked and sat about four chairs away. He took out a notebook and pen to portray that he was taking notes, in case the door opened. She went right into her reason for texting him, "Jasper, we have had a lot of fun, and I want you to know that I am not crazy." Jasper perked up and stopped writing false notes on his notebook. "Now, don't be mad, but I saw something…and…Look, I got your address from your file and stopped by a couple of times." Jasper mouthed the word, *What?* Shelia continued, "I wasn't really stalking you....I was.....umm....just checking you out. That's all."

"So you were stalking me? For how long? Why? What the hell...Seriously..." He felt his voice starting to rise and took a deep breath. There was no need to draw any attention to the room.

"Before you get mad, I got something to tell you...which is why I am admitting this to you. Umm, after you looked sad about the Tina situation, I...umm wanted to come by and make you feel better...I mean check on you. I kept coming by after work trying to get the courage to knock on the door, but I didn't want to seem too infatuated with you. While I was there, I noticed something."

Jasper, at first, thought that she was about to say that saw Vivian or Sonya arrive or leave at his place. His heart thumped with a weird uneasiness. The workplace was not the proper venue to discuss who he was having sex with, even if he was having sex with Shelia from time to time. Those thoughts changed as soon as she said that she noticed something. He started to wonder if she was actually around before the Tina incident and saw her leave the apartment. "What? What did you notice?"

Her look turned to her infamous one of concern that she had been doing a lot lately. "Umm...I wasn't the only one stalking you, as you say." She was hoping that he knew what she was talking about. She was genuinely scared for him. "What is going on with you?"

"What? Huh?" Jasper was clueless, but he figured that Tina had been snooping around his complex for a while. "I can't believe the week that I am having. Wow....just wow!"

She interrupted his mumbling. "Do you know someone with a black Maxima? There was one of those fraternity paddles in the back window, but I am not sure which fraternity." She was shaking at that point. "Well....um...he has been staking out your place too, but I am not sure why."

Jasper felt the room spin as his superior continued to tell him that some big guy was watching him and making periodic phone calls, then leave after a while. He wasn't sure what shocked him more, Shelia or this unknown stalker. He just looked at her in disbelief. He wanted to run to his car to call Rodney to check out the story, but resisted the urge to do so. That phone call would have to wait because Rick was suddenly complaining a lot about the helpdesk personnel talking and hanging out in the hallways too much between trouble tickets.

"Jasper, look, I wanted you to know and to tell you to watch your back." Jasper felt betrayed, but was unsure of who brought on that feeling just then. It may have been Shelia, Tina or the unknown big guy. "We should end this meeting now. I know you are probably mad at me, but I want you to come over later so you can fuss at me there. Ok, baby?" Jasper agreed and noticed that was the first time that Shelia ever called him baby with such sincerity. "I got a couple of other supervisors coming in around 10:30." With that, Jasper poked his head out of the door, saw that the coast was clear and headed back to the helpdesk area.

He sent Rodney a quick email telling him that he needed to talk to him when he got off. He was going to call Kyle when he was on his lunch break. He checked the queue of pending tickets, moved two easy ones to his task list, and sped out of the office. He wasn't in the mood for any of Rick's jokes, questions, or complaints.

The next day, Tim woke up feeling like the time would be soon. After a small conversation on the way home the prior Sunday after watching Jasper's place, the plan changed. He picked up the phone and looked at the time. Feeling lazy on his off day, he decided to take a nap. He hoped that he would have the guts to do what he'd been planning for a while, and new motivation and ideas came from seeing Tina leaving Jasper's apartment in tears.

Approximately 35 minutes later, the alarm on his phone buzzed its annoying tone. Tim stirred slowly, debating on whether he was going to get up and make the call, or continue his nap. In his head, he envisioned Tina in tears again, and he felt justified. He picked up his phone to stop the buzzing and dialed a number that he hadn't called in a while. Tina hesitated when she saw the number, but answered with a cautious, "Hello?"

Tim stuttered, "Hey,,,Tina. What's up? I was calling to...ummm...see how you are doing. Are you...ok?"

Tina, not wanting to relive her mistake of sleeping with him for money, almost hung up the phone. Instead she replied, "Look, we did what we did, but..."

Tim dropped in, "Hey, hey...I ain't calling for that. Look, I...uh...ummm.....whew...ummm......"

Tina subconsciously rolled her eyes, "What Tim? What?" She felt that he was going to try to get her to come over for another round of pay for play, or that he was maybe really trying to date her. She wasn't interested in either one.

Tim took a deep breath to get his words together and blurted out, "Hey, hey...ummm...I saw you at Jasper's crib the other night." He rushed his next words to prevent her from responding. "I know that he hurt you bad. I was only going over there to talk to him when I saw you leaving....crying."

Tina was stunned and confused with why Tim would be over there. She only replied with, "Screw that dude." Those three words were music to Tim's ears. He had no problem approaching her with the rest of the plan after that.

He smiled and lied when he said, "Check this out. I left right after you did because I wasn't expecting to see you there. I called him on the way home, and he was mad disrespectful, mane." Tina half heard him as she remembered how Jasper looked at her nude body with such disdain and disinterest. He continued in his mix of New York and Memphis slang, "I was like, Yo! What the fuck, mane? I called the nigga to squash the shit, and he came at me all stupid and shit!"

He didn't hear Tina responding so he brought up the main point for his phone call. "Yo, I had to hit you up because me and my nigga thought about fucking him up, but I was like "Naw naw son, I like Tina a lil bit, and she might not like that shit." If Tina said anything against what he had said, he would have abandoned the plan and played it off as if he was talking out of anger. He also hoped that she caught the "I like Tina a lil bit" part.

To his delight, she repeated, "Screw that dude." Then to his surprise, she said after that, "I might be able to help you with that."

The two of them talked for about 30 minutes on various ways to set him up. Tina offered up a little money that her mom gave her in order to take Jasper on a romantic getaway. She also gave names of some possible guys that may take the money to help Tim out. They decided to make it look like a robbery attempt, with details like a car with no tags and black clothes to avoid suspicion. They ended the conversation with plans to talk again soon. He attempted to make the next conversation over dinner, but Tina told him that it was not a good idea. "Maybe later."

Kyle called Jasper as soon as he got the word from the Lieutenant Colonel that called him. He only had a few more weeks before he was due to report to Fort Stewart, Georgia. It was typical for commanders to call the students of Army officer training courses after orders of their following assignments were received to welcome them. Lieutenant Colonel Frank Bloomberg said during the conversation with Kyle that he would arrive in time for the training ramp up before his future unit's deployment to Iraq. Though he knew that it was a part of the job, especially after the 9-11 tragedy, it still shocked him to hear that he was going to war.

Jasper only held the phone after Kyle told him the news. He didn't know what to say. He heard the excitement and fear in his friend's voice. He thought back to all of the reports on CNN that he caught a glimpse of. He was sure that Kyle would be fine.

He was that type of guy who you could imagine being a war hero one day. He was dedicated, honest, and knew how to take charge if he had to.

"Yeah, man. They got me, dawg. I am not sure when I am leaving. The date is not set in stone yet." Jasper said a silent prayer for his friend as he held the phone. "I am happy that I will be in Georgia though. Close enough to Atlanta, but not too close." Kyle often referred to himself as a "refined country boy that grew up around Georgia pimps and eating Georgia peaches". By peaches, he was referring to women from Georgia, not the actual fruit. Jasper smiled as he thought about all the times that Kyle would say that line to women or around the fellas.

They talked a few more minutes about Fort Stewart, deploying to Iraq, their careers, and the cute girls in his training course. Avoiding the inevitable, Jasper didn't bring up the Tina episode right away. He could tell it was on his old roommate's mind though. Kyle already knew his thoughts and suddenly said, "I heard that Rodney had no clue about the black car that you were talking about. He is still asking though. Did you call Tina about it?" Kyle had made a couple of inquiring phone calls as well.

"I ain't calling that bitch!" For a while, he suspected Tim, but figured that he wouldn't do anything like stalk him. Then again, he didn't think that he would walk in on him sweating and penetrating Tina either. "I haven't heard from her either. Thank God. "

"So are you worried about this person in the black car? They may not even be there for you. Know what I'm talking about?" Kyle was only worried about his friend overreacting as he was known to do when pushed into a corner. After they got off the phone, he walked over to the window without thinking and looked outside. He didn't see a black car from his view. He closed the blinds and went back to watching television.

Internally, Jasper was fighting a battle that many did not see. Having sex with various women only temporarily subsided the soreness of his heart. He felt that he was getting over the fiasco with Tina, but his trust of people was shattered. The influx of female attention boosted his broken ego somewhat. It really was common for Jasper to sleep on the couch to avoid sleeping in the bed alone. Things had changed.

He lost a little bit of his humanity when he walked in on Tina and Tim that morning. He entered an alternate world at that point. He was then a part of the world where one has to be a player to keep from getting played, where hurt kept you focused and anger kept you from slipping too far into that hurt. He converted from a person who embraced the morning's sunlight and the smile of a passerby, to one who only saw sunlight as a measure of time and warmth and a smile as the face of a hidden meaning. This pseudo-alter-ego kept him in check, sane, or even happy. It might have even aligned his life for better things. Only time would tell.

The new Jasper, no longer disillusioned by love and optimism, had been morphed into a tougher, egotistic, yet broader thinking individual. The same wall that he was building to protect his heart also had the potential to block nourishment for his soul. He often thought if Shelia had been through a similar hurt and was redefined by it. He slowly gained a thorough understanding of her, but he promised himself that he would never be as ice cold as she could be.

Jasper considered calling Tara during what he entitled his recreated hoe phase. He had recently had a conversation with Kyle of how he used to be in his early college years, and he told him shortly after the breakup with Tina, "Dawg, I'ma enjoy this hoe phase for a while. Tina is going to want to come back, but I'ma be like 'Naw…naw'." He realized that Tara genuinely loved him and was not as bourgeois as Tina. He missed how innocent Tara was; he missed her giggle and her smile.

Even at such a young age, he realized that he had an old soul. He had the perspicacity to know that the hoe phase was not for him….not for long anyway. He understood that his recent escapades in the sheets were only going to satisfy him for so long.

That is when he debated on calling Tara or just sending her a text message. He figured that she knew about his split up with Tina by now. It seemed like everyone else knew. Every time he grabbed the phone to call her, memories of how he dogged her at the end of their relationship plagued him. He always ended up putting the phone down. Last he heard, she belonged to DeMarcus now. He always knew DeMarcus wanted to be with her, but he never thought she would go for it. Jasper was wrong, and Tara seemed tainted to him somehow.

Jeffery Hooks was always a man of great perception. His son was simply a younger version of him. He was wise, compassionate and definitely reactive. Over the days following his learning of what Jasper told him about Tina's guest appearance in the apartment, his thoughts turned to daydreams, daydreams turned to dreams and dreams turned to nightmares. He felt compelled to contact Mr. Jackson in an attempt to alleviate any future conflict, but more to ease his own mind. Mr. Jackson wavered on whether he should talk to Mr. Hooks. His wife told him an abridged version of the story, and he knowing his wife, knew deep down that there was something more to the story than she was on letting on.

He answered the phone as if they were old buddies. Mr. Hooks didn't return the warm sentiment and went straight into the point that he called to talk about. "I hate to call you with such a troubled heart and mind, but I am not sure what is going on. First cheating, then breaking and entering…what's next? We love our kids, but I am worried…for both of them."

"Breaking and entering? I don't think that my Tina would do such a thing, but I will support her, right or wrong! That is my daughter, and how dare you call me making her seem like some damn criminal?" He was still shocked, and embarrassed, about Tina leaving the apartment because of what she did. He was just as embarrassed about his plan to motivate her productivity and possibly being a catalyst to what transpired. He heard rumblings about Tina trying to get Jasper back, but he stayed out of it. He had no idea about Tina breaking into Jasper's apartment or anything else. He really did not want to know.

The two fathers went back and forth for a few minutes. Both were cruelly defending their children and what they only knew partial information about. It ended with Mr. Jackson hanging up after screaming in a higher octave voice than normal, "Good day to you!"

Jasper's mom caught the last bit of the conversation and stood quietly in the hallway, not announcing her presence. Shocked at being hung up on, Mr. Hooks mumbled, "Oh hell naw! You ol' high society, punk muthafucka!"

Chapter 21

Jasper understood that his job was really a thankless one for the most part, and he was not the braggadocios type that needed validation for his daily accomplishments. He was learning, and he had a lot more to learn. He was making waves and receiving a lot of positive feedback from those in the building. Therefore he was truly shocked when he was called sternly by Rick, "Mr. Hooks, I need to see you."

Jasper was very bright and learned things very quickly. Anything that he couldn't just pick up, he focused on and dedicated time to learning. He wasn't the type that grew up with computers at an early age or made programs just for fun on weekends. Back in college, he was the type of student who didn't really study hard because he just picked up his subjects and got to a reasonable amount of understanding before the tests. He wasn't going to be the type that had a garage full of old computer gear that he built and experimented with over the years. He was the type that would always be socially capable as well as technically competent in his career. He was not really concerned about being the best in his field or better than the next guy. He was taught to do more than what was needed of him and in an exceedingly well manner.

Jasper walked over to Rick's large section in the helpdesk area and took a seat. Rick kept typing away at an email while Jasper sat quietly looking at all the junk accumulated around his desk. "Yes sir?" Rick still didn't say anything, but he turned to look him in the eyes before he kept typing. Jasper was trying not to look irritated, but he felt Rick was up to something.

Finally, Rick stopped typing and asked, "How many trouble tickets did you finish today?" Jasper looked at his watch and wondered why that question was asked. He arrived slightly before 9 that morning, and his watch read 10:47.

In response, he said, "I've done three, and I have…" Rick stopped his explanation with faltering sternness in his voice, "Three, huh? I just replied to an email from Mr. Jason Peterson on the 3rd floor. He says that you spend a lot of time in his vicinity chatting away. You know we are backed up."

Flabbergasted, Jasper shook his head and said, "What?" with perhaps a little too much revulsion. "Yo, sir. I talk to Mr. Wilson about sports every blue moon, and I was only down there a few minutes today. I have been stuck troubleshooting another computer on that floor all morning. I spoke to him as the computer was restarting, then I got back to work." Rick only looked at him as if he had robbed a bank and was lying about it.

It was obvious that his immediate supervisor was just waiting on anything semi-relevant to blast Jasper about. He felt targeted even though his indiscretion was minor. He knew that retaliation was expected after Shelia overheard their conversation that one day. He felt that Rick was trying to incite anger and disrespect to come from him just so he would have something more serious to snap about. His dad always told him, "Bite your tongue. They want you to get mad so you look like a stereotypical angry black man."

"Look Jasper. I know you feel popular and maybe even like a superstar, but this is a place of business. Get Mr. Wilson's number to talk about sports. You represent the helpdesk, and we are always professional. You got that." One of the other helpdesk members slowed down her walk to eavesdrop on the conversation. Jasper glared at her, and she walked on. "Report back to me when you finish that trouble ticket down there."

His face was uncontrollably contorted in a fuming frown, but Jasper just said, "Ok, I got ya. I am about to go back down there right now." He didn't wait to be dismissed and hurried toward the office door. Sounding just like his father, Jasper said under his breath, "Ok. Game on, bitch." just as the door closed.

He bypassed the elevators and ran down the stairs to get outside of the InfoTech Solutions front doors. His heart was beating rapidly. He wanted to punch something. He wanted to slap Rick for hiding his true feelings behind some weak legitimacy. He looked toward the parking lot and had a moment of clarity. After that, he knew what to do.

He went back to the third floor and resumed working. As Mr. Wilson walked in with a refilled coffee mug, Jasper purposely said loudly, "Mr. Wilson, you done did it now."

He stopped in mid sip, confused, and said back, "Come again."

Jasper got up and walked closer to Jason Peterson's cubicle. "Yes sir. I just got in major trouble because I lollygag too much down here and don't do enough work."

He hoped that the plan would work out as he envisioned it. Mr. Wilson, an older gentleman, had been working at InfoTech Solutions just as long as Rick and was known to be somewhat militant. Mr. Peterson was timid and soft-spoken, and one would wonder his sexuality if it wasn't for the family photos taped and pinned around his workspace. Mr. Wilson, as expected, put his mug down and said, "Who the hell said that shit? Huh? I know your boss ain't talking that noise as much as he runs around here talking to everybody all day, every day."

Jasper knew who had said it, but said, "I don't know, sir. I don't know. It's ok though."

"No, it is not ok. You come down and talk to me, but you are the one who always cut it short so you can go back to work. I'm going go talk to his shaggy ass right now. Now, he is picking on the new blood up in here."

As Mr. Wilson went on and on, Mr. Peterson slowly stood up, as if on cue, looking frightened. He was the Division chairman and Mr. Wilson's supervisor. He spoke in his usual nasally, whispered voice, "Hey fellas. I'm the one that sent the email." Jasper looked over at Mr. Wilson who was staring furiously at his supervisor.

Seeing that, Mr. Peterson quickly threw in, "Mr. Rick from the helpdesk came down here a couple of weeks ago and asked me to keep track of how long he was down here. I sent him an email last week saying that you guys just talk about sports every so often. That's all. I thought it was weird, but I was like, 'Ok.'" He waived his hands around dramatically and almost sang the word, "Ok".

It was all falling into place. He knew that Mr. Wilson would have his back and hoped that Mr. Peterson would squeal and not want to cause any trouble. In the process, he confirmed that his supervisor was just fishing to get him on something, even if he had to stretch the truth. "Sir, Rick said that you sent it today. Do you think I am disruptive, sir?"

His mouth dropped upon being asked that, and an animated gasp sounded. "Now that's a bold-faced lie there, Mr. Hooks." He placed his hands on his hips and continued, "There is nothing wrong with having a little convo around the office…as long as work is being done. Umm…hmm. I listen to your little sport talks, and I only have one thing that I would like to say…Go Bears."

They all laughed which eased the tension, and the chatter proved that Rick was up to something. It would be suspicious if he told Shelia because he knew that she would confront Rick. He decided to keep what he learned to himself until he was pushed into a corner. He sadly realized that he would have to be on his best behavior. Also, he was going to start looking at other positions within the company. He would ask Shelia about it one day after they finished their usual routine.

A couple of days later, Rodney was leaving a meeting that a couple of the band members requested to discuss the situation of the absent lead singer and checked his text messages while walking back to his car. Ironically, he saw a message from his ex-girlfriend who left Pembrook before graduating to pursue her singing career. Without reading it, he erased it. There was one from his wife asking him to bring some chicken breasts and a few other things home after his meeting. The last was from one of his frat brothers reporting that he had checked into the black car and found nothing.

He was about to call Jasper to discuss his findings when another text message came in from his ex-girlfriend followed by a phone call. He ignored both and turned off his phone before proceeding to a store near his house. While the phone was off, another one of his frat brothers (known as Sledgehammer to most of his friends) called back with some information that he just received. Rodney never got the information since the phone was off. He didn't turn on the phone until much later after he gave his daughter a bath and worked on some music that he wanted the band to try. He saw that he had a couple of voice messages, but didn't listen to them.

Chapter 22

Shelia's revelation shook Jasper more than he thought it would. Thoughts constantly churned in his head. *Why would someone be spying on me? Was it Tina or one of her girlfriends? No, Sheila said that it was a guy in that car. It couldn't be Rick because she said there was a fraternity paddle in the car. Tim would be foolish enough to come back for another ass-whooping. Sonya didn't seem like the type that had stalkers. Maybe Shelia just thought that she saw something strange as she was stalking her damn self.*

One particular day, the thoughts circled in his head as he sipped the last bit of his third beer. Something didn't feel right with the situation and all that he had going on. He felt even crazier that his urge to drink increased, even on weekdays. He wasn't worried about it getting out of control, but the alcohol gave him some sense of calm. Maybe it was all in his head. His heart thumped one day when he was checking the mail and a black car drove by. The driver was an older man whose mind was nowhere near thinking about Jasper. He considered getting a few games for his Playstation 2 console to give himself something else to occupy his time. He went to the refrigerator to grab another beer and saw that he was out. "Damn."

His TV was on, but it was watching him more than he was watching it, as his dad would say. One would see the young man sitting alone on the couch staring in space with empty bottles lined up nearby, like someone going through some sort of depression. He was just coming into his manhood and all of the responsibilities, joys, struggles, and pain that being a man would bring. Paying bills, job-related stress, women problems, and a broken heart, among other things were just the beginning of what he would have to go through.

In his thoughts that day, he considered calling Tara again. He dialed all of the numbers except the last one. Again, he stopped himself from going through with it. *What would I say to her? Why didn't she ever call me?* He deleted the numbers and closed his phone. With his eyes closed, he sat there playing movies of true passion in his head. He knew that he really made a mistake. As he reflected, he eventually started to feel numb, yet tortured at the same time. His soul succumbed to the numbness with all that he had going on. To break his somber mood and dismal attitude, he decided to make a surprise visit to his parents' house to see what they had cooked for dinner.

Delphina Hooks had just finished putting up the food on the stove when there was a knock on the door. She recognized the way that her son always knocked before using his key to open the door. She walked toward the front and yelled, "Boy, what if me and your dad were naked on the couch? You barely gave us enough time to get dressed."

She met her son in the living room with a look of disgust on his face. "Mom, really? Yuck. Don't talk like that." They both laughed and embraced. "Mom, what's for dinner? Where's dad at?" Without waiting on an answer, he rushed into the kitchen. He could smell the lingering aroma of the chicken breasts that she chopped up and fried, as well as that of yellow rice which his dad loved. He fixed a plate as his mom said that Mr. Hooks was taking a nap. Jasper placed the plate in the microwave and went upstairs to look in on his dad, to see if he was still sleep.

He entered the room hearing the thunderous snoring that he grew up listening to. He walked in, closed the door, and tiptoed toward the closet. He liked to borrow some of his father's dress shirts, ties, and other things from time to time. He slowly opened the door, peeked in a couple of boxes and placed something in his pocket. He slowly closed the door back and left the room. He walked in his old room to get his old paintball gun. He slid the item in his pocket into the box and left. He joined his mom back downstairs and retrieved the plate of food from the microwave. They talked about work, and she eventually brought up the phone call between his dad and Tina's dad earlier in the week. Jasper not wanting to discuss it only continued eating.

After the meal and more conversation, Jasper thanked his mom and told her that he needed to head home to get ready for work. The visit made Jasper feel so much better, and his mom knew that the visit was for more than just food. The therapeutic nature of their conversations always warmed her heart. This was something that was even true when he was very little, and his conversations were more about fantasy creatures and filled with what if questions. She hugged his neck and allowed it to linger a few seconds for both of their sakes. She wanted him to feel loved and she needed to feel that he would be ok.

Tina woke up most mornings feeling absolute anger after she attempted to reconcile with Jasper. The embarrassment she felt incited more rage every day. The way she saw the situation was that she made a terrible mistake, and she felt terrible for it. She was truly sorry about her indiscretions and was ready to spend a lifetime making up for them as long as he gave her a chance. The problem was that he didn't give her a chance and laughed at her as he refused her. She held back some tears as she stepped in the shower thinking, *He did not have to laugh at me like that!*

She promised two guys that were former classmates of hers that she would give them $150 each to scare Jasper and punch him a couple of times, if necessary. They were to join Tim in the effort to teach him a lesson. She originally asked three guys, but one said that he didn't want to be involved. She also promised to meet Tim for lunch to discuss the final details. She dreaded the decision to meet him in person, but she had to make sure that all was going to occur according to plan. Ever since they reconnected, he was constantly trying to get her to hang out and dropped insinuations about dating.

She got dressed and headed out the door. She texted the two guys that agreed to be a part of the plot to make sure they were still willing to participate. Each one of them agreed and asked questions about times, places, and payment. Tina smiled as she envisioned her ex-boyfriend's face as three guys rushed him, threatened him, robbed him, and gave him a message.

When she pulled up to the meeting spot she sighed as she saw Tim's grin widen. She got out of the car, spewing attitude and acting like she had to be somewhere soon. Though she accepted her fault in what came to light, seeing him only reminded her of her stupidity and greed. She acted out against him sometimes unintentionally in their interactions.

Tim attempted a hug, which she innocently waived off when she went to sit on the bench along the Memphis Riverfront.

There was a little seating area near Mud Island that had somewhat of a private feel to it. They sat in an awkward silence for a minute that Tina quickly broke with talk of the plan. "So how are we going to do this? Let me hear how you see it."

Tim saw a different Tina than the one that he used to lust over. Even during their financially motivated affair, she still acted with decency and smiled. He shrugged the urge to ask how she was doing and replied, "See, I see it like this. We wait until he is about to go to work. There will not be too many people outside, I guess. Me and your boys roll up on him wearing black and get him to apologize for hurting you. Then you come up to hear him apologize to you personally. Then we roll out." Tina's eyes were wide with disbelief as he gave his simplistic and unsophisticated plan. He continued, "He should be scared by that point and do it. If he doesn't, we can give him a couple of uppercuts to the gut. Ya feel me, ma?"

When he finished, they sat there in the same awkward silence. Tina had to consciously close her mouth to not make Tim feel like he was idiot. She cleared her throat and said, "Ok. I feel you, but....Ok. Check this out. How about we make it look like a robbery attempt instead?" He looked up with interest. "Tim, how about you guys roll up on him with masks and rob him? You can get in a lick or two, and tell him that he shouldn't do people wrong...kinda like he had it coming to him. He will think about it and reflect on some things. Maybe he will even call me to apologize."

Tim winced when she mentioned Jasper calling her to apologize. "Why would you want to be with him after all of that shit he did to you? Huh? Maybe you should find someone that will treat you better than that, you know?"

Tina rolled her eyes and bluntly spat out, "Boy, I already told you that you and I can't date. It will be too weird." She giggled, then said, "You and I are cool, and what happened, happened. It was wrong, and we got caught."

"Wait just a fucking minute, Ms. Thang! You called me up. You were the one that told me how much you needed money and wanted to get fucked. You said that it was cool to come to your place, and I drove to Memphis all early in the morning each time. Don't blame me for how it all turned out. Shit, at least you didn't get punched." The crazed look in Tim's eyes scared Tina, and she suddenly valued him a little more. He was right….she was the one that got them into the situation.

"When you needed money, I was there. Boom. When he kicked you out, I was there. Boom. I am here now. Boom!" He looked for a reaction from Tina, who just stared again with her mouth open. "Aight Tina? Let's just do this shit and get it over with. Let's finish up with the plan." He felt stupid for liking her while they attended Pembrook. He regretted opening up his apartment to her after he got beat up. He hated not having a love of his own instead of chasing someone infatuated with her past.

After yet another awkward pause, they finalized the details of the plan. Tim would be the driver of the getaway car on the other side of the complex near the exit. Jasper might recognize him or his voice, so the other two would do the robbery. If it went smoothly, he would leave Tina in the car, and she could join them to get a kick or smack in. The three guys would have masks on to hide their faces so Jasper would not know who attacked him. The apartment complex didn't have any cameras, and Tina would be nearby to stand as lookout.

They went back and forth with details of the plan. They agreed on wearing all black and where to park the car. They decided that Sunday before Jasper went to church, if he went that day, would be best since traffic around the apartments would be less compared to a morning as people went to school or work. Tim was astonished by Tina's attention to detail and how thoroughly she had plotted all of the details they were discussing even prior to their meeting. Tina was almost fearful that Tim couldn't get past his rage and desire for revenge enough to follow the plan. He constantly grunted and made fists as he spoke.

After 45 minutes of discussing everything, silence plagued them again. There was really no more to discuss. Tina had to relay the plan to the guys willing to help, and Tim had to do a final recon of the apartment complex to solidify what was discussed. Tina smiled as she looked Tim in the eyes and said, "Ok, Tim. I will talk to you a lil later. Ok?" She gave him an elongated embrace. She could fill his tension loosen as they hugged. She smiled and said, "Thanks", as they let go. Her smile faded instantly as she turned and walked toward her car. She knew that it behooved her to act like she was at least friendly when around him, to keep him involved and focused.

Chapter 23

Jasper slowly became fed up with Sonya's complaints for more time. He was mentally worn-out with only seeing Shelia late at night at her place or expensive hotel rooms. He was also tired of having to act like he barely knew her at work. He always felt like he was looking over his shoulder at InfoTech. Vivian's texts asking for another round of sex were starting to be ignored. There were women that he had met recently that were wondering if they would ever get another phone call. Tina started texting again with apologies, and those were being ignored as always. Lastly, the woman that he wanted to talk to still hadn't made an effort to contact him, nor did he have the courage to make an effort to contact her.

Jasper was enjoying the freedom to taste as many exotic flavors on his analogical wall of shaved ice flavors. One could say that he was trying out too many flavors at one time. Some would say that it was perfectly normal for a young, single man to taste until he found his favorite flavor. Most would agree that too many flavors usually do not mix well. The sweetness or the tartness of each brings its own unique flavor, but mixing too many may only leave a murky mess that may taste sweet at first and possibly give you a bellyache later.

Jasper's bellyache was a mixture of heartache and being emotionally drained. His walk in youthful, carefree fantasy had sprouted roots in reality. The dangerous path that he walked started to bring more risk and confusion than rewards. Morality and common sense crept into his conscious for he knew that it was only a matter of time before someone's feelings were deeply hurt, he was caught by someone, or a possibility of worse developments that he was not ready for.

Those close to him, especially those intimately close to him, noticed a difference in the demeanor of the always happy Jasper Hooks over the past couple of weeks. It was late August, and Jasper was quite a different person from who he was the day he graduated college. His exciting and eventful summer matured him quickly from his juvenile former self. There was nothing alarming though, because life events are supposed to be learning experiences.

One particular week, Jasper was in a state of bewilderment at work. He constantly seemed lost in his thoughts, whether sitting at his desk or during the many meetings he attended. Even Rick mentioned to him that he seemed like he was not getting sufficient sleep. Instead of being comforting and encouraging, Rick looked at his state as an opportunity to ensue confrontation.

On Wednesday of that particular week, Rick stopped Jasper as he was leaving the helpdesk to go to the restroom. In his typical sarcastic nature, he tapped Jasper on the shoulder and asked, "What do you have going on right now?"

Jasper didn't realize that he had scowled in return before replying, "I am working on those mandatory training modules….about to take a quick bathroom break."

He started to walk away, but Rick asked, "Did you knock out a few tickets before you started your training?"

Jasper saw that he was trying to get a rise out of him and wanted to stop it before it got there, so he asked back "Sir, why is it that you seem to be picking on me? There are no critical tickets that need addressing and everyone else is chilling around the corner." The room was built with a wall that only surrounded Rick's office area. The rest of the employees sat in an open area behind some partitions. Laughter could be heard as someone was cracking a joke. Rick obviously heard it, but focused on messing with the subordinate standing in front of him.

It was obvious that Rick was still acting out of the embarrassment Shelia made him feel from past interactions, though a lot of time had passed since then. Shelia never was the type to make harsh comments or abuse her position, but she felt the need to have a thorough conversation with Rick after watching his interaction with Jasper that day in the hallway. At the time, Rick only suspected of a relationship that hadn't occurred yet. Shelia's talk with him was both misdirection and a verbal counseling session for his disrespectful comments.

Shelia rubbed his ego when she said, "All of us owe you for the times that you updated our servers and computers, or the times you keep us from going crazy as you recovered data as we made stupid mistakes because we didn't know what we are doing on these computers." Rick smiled proudly as she made that comment. "If you have an issue with me, let's talk about it. My door is always open for that. If you are simply picking on Jasper or anybody else, stop it. You know the proper way to advise your people against insubordination." He took the last part of that statement too literal. He had nothing on his star employee, but he was setting up the dominoes for Jasper to knock down.

As Jasper stood there with his fists balled up, Rick recalled that previous conversation. "Shelia told me to stop picking on you that one day, and I think that you are fucking her. Yeah, that is it." Jasper looked around to see if anyone else was nearby, and he was thankful that no one was. The humming of the servers in the room covered the conversation.

"No, Ms. Bunton just sees that you are picking on me, and I do not understand why. Sir, I do my job, and I go home. She is cute and all, but she is too old me for me. The question is, are you fucking her?" The suddenly flustered face of his supervisor spoke utter embarrassment and annoyance.

Jasper purposely said the last part of his statement louder than he had to with the purpose of trying to sound louder than the humming of the equipment. He said it as a way to turn the conversation around by directing the accusations towards Rick or to attract the attention of his coworkers to come around the corner to nosily see what was transpiring. Rick's reaction was totally unexpected. Jasper saw that he actually might have been attracted to Shelia, and he had to hold back his laughter. As two other helpdesk employees came around the corner, Rick screamed out, "You little think-you-know-it-all little bastard!"

Will Cox, who sat at the desk next to Jasper, stared in disbelief of what he just heard. "Oh shit." The encounter ended with Will pulling Jasper into the hallway after their boss almost lunged at him. Unfriendly words like "racist hippie" and "young punk" were screamed in the heavily air conditioned room before the two hot-headed men were separated. Jasper felt that it was best to just go home after that. He planned on going to Shelia's boss the next day to report his side of the story since the issue involved her name. He also did not want to get her involved too much at that point. There was no proof that he had been with her, and he had enough witnesses to Rick's erratic behavior to spark a viable harassment investigation.

Shelia called him later that evening as he was getting tipsy and convinced him to let the incident go without reporting it to anyone. Rick was persuaded to take the rest of the week off. She also attempted to ease his mind by offering a massage or to join him for a drink. He jumped in and cut off her appealing proposal. He spent the rest of the night playing his video games until his eyes started to close on their own.

The rest of the week at work was normal for Jasper. His days pretty much consisted of doing his job, avoiding any discussion of the episode with his coworkers, and spending his nights playing video games. He had no desire to have any female company and turned down any requests that came his way. Friday night into Saturday morning, he stayed up playing one of his video games, attempting to get past a difficulty level.

While Jasper was killing zombies on his TV that Saturday, Tim was talking to DeMarcus to see if he would like to get involved in the plan that he had devised with Tina. "Check it out, son. It is foolproof. He ain't going to know what happened to him. He ain't going to know that it is us. Ya feel me? Make that muthafucka think that he ain't that hot shit he thinks he is. Ya feel me?"

DeMarcus, who was on board when it was first presented to him weeks ago, was totally against it as Tim rambled on and on. "Man, that's our frat brother."

Tim sneered as he barked, "Man, fuck Jasper!"

They both argued their points on why it was ok versus why it was so wrong. The squabble concluded as DeMarcus said, "Bruh, I am good. I don't think that you should do it, and I will act like I didn't hear you say anything about this shit." Tim made DeMarcus promise to keep his mouth shut, and he agreed. "Aight bruh…I just don't want anything to do with it."

After a pang of guilt and much internal debate, DeMarcus decided to call Tara hours later saying that he needed to desperately talk to her. She saw his number and ignored it. After he attempted twice, she turned off her phone. He sat on his balcony cursing her name. He prayed for forgiveness for even considering hurting Jasper, and he hoped that Tim changed his mind. After failing to reach Tim in a final effort to dissuade him, he attempted to call Tara again and hung up once her voicemail greeting started. He looked in his phone contacts hoping that he had Kyle's number. He took a deep breath and hit the Call button once he found it. Kyle was in his Army lodging suite enjoying the company of one of the women attending the same course as him. He was too busy to hear his phone ring or even care.

Chapter 24

It was already a hot summer Sunday morning in Memphis and only due to get hotter. The moisture of the Mississippi River was contributing to the stuffy feeling in the air. It was quite unbearable by 8 a.m. and would dry one's eyes or crack dry lips as soon you walked out of your front door.

Tim woke up early that morning on his brother's couch despite drinking and partying with him just hours prior. Tim borrowed his brother's black car again, claiming that he didn't want the girl that he was messing around with in Memphis to know his real car. The lie worked each time that he wanted to do a recon around Jasper's neighborhood.

After the car swap, he picked up Tina and the two guys at a nearby Wal-Mart. He instantly recognized the two as some of Tina's frat brothers. One was known around Pembrook College as Skeelo, and the other was nicknamed Big James. They both graduated before Tina or Tim, but he remembered seeing them around the yard or during a homecoming weekend. After a quick reacquainting, they loaded up in the borrowed black Nissan

Maxima. Tina gave a quick review of everyone's role as they headed toward the apartment complex. Everyone seemed slightly nervous, but Skeelo cracked jokes which calmed everyone down somewhat.

On the other side of town, Jasper remained still halfway sleep on his couch debating on whether he was going to make it to church that morning. Sleep would easily welcome him back after a rather sleepless night. His fatigue at that moment was more than physical. Mentally, he was tired from thinking too much about his recent events. His spirit was drained from the disappointment and aggravation he felt. Physically, he was tired from his late nights playing video games in an attempt to sooth his thoughts.

He was motivated by getting some of his mother's cooking as he rolled out of his bed in his underwear. He looked out of the window and saw nothing out of the ordinary. No strange black car in sight. He sent his mom a text message before he got in the shower saying that he was running late, but that he would meet her soon. He slowly got dressed, contemplating on reneging on meeting his mom at church.

Kyle woke up lying next to the young lady that he had spent all weekend with. She ignored his advances to get some late morning affection, so he hopped out of bed to use the bathroom and get some orange juice. He looked at his phone and noticed that he had three voicemails that he had ignored the day prior. He turned on his speakerphone and placed the phone on the counter as he went to get a glass for his juice.

The first voicemail was from one of his other classmates, commenting about his early departure from a barbeque Friday night with the woman who was actually in his bedroom. He laughed and deleted the message. The next one almost made him choke on the juice that he was sipping on. The voice he heard was that of DeMarcus frantically begging for him to call Jasper. "Bruh, bruh, bruh!! This is DeMarcus, man. Call me....As soon, as soon....As you hear this. That nigga Tim is tripping, man. He came by the crib today talking about robbing Jasper. He ain't going to believe me, man. Call me back and tell Jasper to watch out." The rest of the message was his phone number and more pleads for a call back.

Kyle was frozen holding his glass, and an ocean of thoughts were flowing in his mind. The automated female voice coming out of his phone was prompting him to hit certain numbers to delete, repeat, or save the message. He pressed the number corresponding to repeating the message and listened again carefully. Curiosity and skepticism stopped him from taking action as he listened to the next message. DeMarcus had sent another frantic message. "Kyle, man, I need you to holla back at me. I told Tim not to do that shit, but he said that Tina already had everything set up."

He hung the phone at that point and called Jasper. His corny voicemail message played because he was in the shower during the time of the call. Kyle called again and panicked. The young lady yawned as she walked out his room, "What's wrong, K?" He thought that he was too late to warn Jasper.

"I think my old roomie is in trouble." Being so far away, he felt hopeless. He called Rodney since he was a lot closer to Jasper.

Rodney was getting ready to get in the car with Katrina, his daughter, and his bass guitar. He was going to play with the choir at the popular First Baptist Church that he periodically attended since his sophomore year at Pembrook. "What up, pimp?" He answered the phone expecting just some regular catch up talk from his former roommate. The concern in Kyle's voice scared him.

"Hey mane! Have you heard from Jasper today?" Kyle sounded more frantic than DeMarcus did in his warning voicemails. He quickly recapped what he heard and screamed at

Rodney to do something. "I think that you need to drive to Memphis and check on him. He is not picking up the fucking phone." Rodney remained calm and asked his wife to go on to church without him and apologize to the pastor for him because he had an emergency. Katrina complied with no argument. Her husband's face showed deep trouble and that he was in no mood to answer any questions.

Rodney attempted to calm Kyle down, which was so unlike their natures. Usually, it was Kyle who had to calm down aggressive and loud Rodney. "Look pimp. I need you to calm the fuck down and keep calling Jasper. I sent Katrina to church, so I'm going make a few phone calls.

Kyle simply said, "Aight" and hung up. He apologized to his lady friend. "Hey, I gotta handle this. You can stay if you want to, but excuse me while I make a few phone calls." Then he did just as Rodney told him and attempted to call Jasper again.

Rodney was stung with the fact that he never called his homeboy who was looking into the mysterious black car that Jasper was told about. He texted Katrina with a quick update then called him to see what he knew before he made some other phone calls. "Dude, answer your fucking phone! I tried talking to you about the black car thing. I heard on the low that his boy Tim was trying to recruit people to beat Jasper up or something. When I didn't hear from you I figured that you already knew or something."

"Naw. I wished you would've called back, but it's all good. Thanks mane! I'ma hit you up later." They talked for two more minutes before ending the call. Rodney took off his tie and sat on his couch. He hoped that Kyle was able to reach Jasper. He hoped that they were just overacting and worried for nothing.

The black car was in position in the apartment complex. The two older guys hopped out of the car with Tina who showed them the apartment where Jasper stayed. It was very quiet in the neighborhood with only a few people stirring around. There were not enough people to even be suspicious of two guys and a girl wearing all black walking around.

Tim sat in the car alone with a funny feeling in the gut of his stomach. It was too late to back out now, and he only hoped that things went smoothly. After DeMarcus chopped into him for going through with it, he thought about it several times. He was angry at Jasper for kicking his ass, but he would have done the same thing if Tina, or any woman, was cheating on him with another man for money. He shifted through memories of his times with Tina, physically and in conversation, and questioned if he was being used for his affections toward her. Regardless, it was too late to run away from it all.

Tina walked quickly with Big James and Skeelo whispering last minute bailout plans if they were seen or if things went awry. Big James calmly smoked a cigarette while Skeelo nervously shuffled his hands in his pocket. When in place, Tina walked across the street to her designated spot and pulled out her cell phone. From her vantage point, she would see Jasper before he saw her. Also, she could call the guys if they happened to miss Jasper as he went to the car or it seemed like he wasn't going to church.

Skeelo tapped his partner in crime on the shoulder and showed him the knife that he was carrying. Big James gasped as Skeelo stated, "We don't know this nigga. This is just in case he wears his big boy draws today." Big James chuckled and said, "Man, let's just scare this fool and get on."

Jasper was a creature of habit and predicatively stepped out of his apartment around 10:47 a.m. to make it to his mother's church by 11:30. Big James looked up first as he heard the door open on the second floor. The two men looked around, put on their ski masks and crept toward the steps. The plan was to catch Jasper by surprise as he walked down the stairs. From a distance, Tina was able to see the whole thing and blinked when she thought that she saw something shiny come out of Skeelo's pocket.

Jasper was aloof to what was going on and turned around as he reached the stairs remembering that he left his Bible in the apartment. He yawned as he turned the key and re-entered his place. Thinking that he was going to be in and out, he left the door cracked open and the key inside the lock. Skeelo was anxious and pushed past his cohort to run up the stairs. Big James followed suit and Tina silently said, "Oh shit!"

Jasper was only back inside his place for twelve seconds when he heard some shuffling and his door slam. He dropped the book in his hand when he rushed out of his bedroom to see two guys that looked like they spent much time in the gym wearing all black and masks. He noticed one coming at him with a rather large knife who said, "Listen up, bitch. Don't say anything. Don't scream like the bitch you are, and we ain't gotta hurt you. Aight?" Jasper looked at the other one whose eyes seemed to be opened with more surprise than his own. He nodded in agreement and raised his hands in surrender.

Tina couldn't see anything happening from where she was standing and quickly became concerned. She called Tim sounding terrified. "Those idiots fucked up the plan and ran into his apartment! Oh shit….damn." She sat on the bench near her and Tim asked whether or not he should come see what was happening. She sharply said, "No, stay in the damn car."

He sat there sitting in the car feeling completely like an idiot. His original plan was to get Jasper alone and unsuspectingly get him back for their encounter months ago. All that changed when he told his plan to Tina. It was painfully obvious to him that she wasn't into him the way that he wished she was. *How the hell I make a plan and end up being the fucking driver?* He seriously thought about leaving, but it would be wrong to leave the other three there. He thought about getting out and walking over to see what was going on, but he needed to be ready to leave when and if the guys came running back. The funny feeling returned in his stomach twice as bad. He laughed to keep from throwing up. He laughed at himself for being so stupid.

Inside the apartment, masked man #1, Skeelo, was barking at Jasper and at masked man #2, Big James. Visibly, Jasper was quite scared. He would have tried his hand at knocking out at least one of the guys, but the blade of the knife pointed at him made him reconsider. He was made to turn around and face his bedroom and told to put his hands on the pull-up bar hanging on the door frame. He overheard the second masked guy whispering to the first asking him, "What the fuck are you doing? This wasn't the plan."

Skeelo glowered to his companion and whispered too loudly, "If we are going to do this shit, let's get something more than $150 dollars."

Jasper felt a flurry of emotions ranging from fear to anger to confusion. He tried to look over his shoulder to gauge his distance from his dining room table. He felt a hard push in the area of his back near the left kidney and was met with heated words. "Nigga, I told you that we don't want to hurt your sorry ass. Somebody doesn't like you and want us to fuck you up." Jasper instantly thought about the puzzle of the black car. The rookie mugger kept talking. "Me and my partner here are businessmen. You give us enough money and we will let you be, bruh. You hear me, bitch?" Jasper could smell the scent of the gum that the guy was chewing he was so close to his ear.

Kyle couldn't be consoled by the nude body talking to him. He was sick with worry and pissed at himself for not checking his phone earlier. He paced in his boxer shorts constantly calling Jasper, which there was no answer. He called Rodney to get an update. "Yo, I called Sonya. She doesn't stay too far from him. She said that she would go by his crib to check on him." The news made Kyle feel better, but not satisfied. Rodney continued, "Playa, I'ma call DeMarcus to get some background on this shit. You think we should call Daddy Hooks?"

He swallowed some more juice before answering. Kyle had the same thought initially, but did not want to even go that route. There was a chance that Jasper's dad was at church with his wife, but he often opted to stay at home. Kyle hoped that was the case that day as he said, "I'll call him." After one last attempt to contact Jasper, Kyle made a hesitant phone call to the Hooks residence.

Mr. Hooks answered on the third ring sounding like an older version of his son. "Hello." Kyle stammered through a rundown of what was going on and what they had done thus far in trying to reach him. "What you say there, boy?" The news almost made the father faint, and he looked to see if his wife noticed because he knew she would overreact and realized that she was already at church. "So you haven't heard from him? Damn it! This ain't no joke, is it?"

Kyle was almost in tears as he choked out the words, "I wish this was a joke, sir."

Jeffrey Hooks hung up the phone and shuffled up the stairs up to his bedroom closet. He bent over and opened up the small hard-shelled suitcase where he kept his two guns. He almost fainted again as he realized that his .45 caliber pistol was not in its usual storage place. Jasper had indeed made up a reason to come by the other day. His wife stated something about him leaving with his old paintball gun as he slept. He prayed out loud, "Lord, please protect my son....and protect the muthafucka that crosses him." He grabbed the 9mm in the suitcase and an extra magazine loaded with hollow point ammo.

Just for verification, he walked into Jasper's old room and looked in the closet. He instantly saw the paintball gun sitting on the floor without the box. He grabbed a jacket and shuffled back down the stairs. He got in his car, closed his eyes to say another prayer, and departed the driveway to get to Jasper's apartment as quickly as traffic would allow.

Skeelo and Big James still had their masks on as they emptied out a box and had Jasper toss his wallet and watch in it. Skeelo kept the knife on him as Big James looked around his room for more valuables. Big James, the smaller of the two guys, was fumbling in his closet cursing quietly under his breath. Something felt strange about the robbery attempt. It was as if he was the one being robbed instead of Jasper.

He saw that he had to make an opportunity before it was too late. He slowly slid his hands across the bar toward the door frame. He felt another blow to his lower back. "Why are you moving, bitch?" Jasper held himself up and adjusted his hands to the edges of the bar. He yelled in pain which made Skeelo adjust his stance in order to shut him up. He walked up to Jasper's ear again. "Shut up, bitch! Shush that shit. You hear me?" That was just enough time for Jasper to quickly lift the straight, chrome bar up about two inches outside of the braces holding it in place.

As the man with knife stepped back to where he was standing, he looked up in time to see Jasper drop his left hand, duck, and spin around swing the bar in his right hand. Skeelo jumped back toward the couch as Jasper missed him with the wild swing. He almost dropped the knife as he recovered, while Jasper darted toward the paintball gun box sitting on the small dining room table. As Skeelo prepared to swing the knife he was yielding, he froze when saw the box drop to the floor, and the captive pointing his father's gun at him.

"No, you shush that shit, big dude." Big James walked out of the room and dropped the box that he was carrying. Watches, cologne bottles and many other items fell out of the box when he threw his arms in the air. "Naw, don't look scared now! Both of you get down on your knees." Big James complied without hesitation while his partner stood frozen with a tightened smile on his face and knife still in his hand.

"This is not a game, big timer. Drop the damn knife, or I will shoot that shit out of your hands." Jasper was screaming because he was so pissed about getting attacked in his own apartment for some reason unknown to him. He would have pulled that trigger if the bigger of the two guys made a wrong move. He thought that the smaller one was Tim until he started talking.

Big James didn't seem as big, as he whimpered about how they shouldn't have done this shit. He punched Skeelo in the leg and said with sheer fear in his voice, "Nigga, get your crazy ass down before I get shot fucking with you." Skeelo dropped the knife, and Jasper almost pulled the trigger as a reaction.

As Skeelo got down on his knees, Jasper shouted to him, "You lay all the way down….hands flat muthafucka." He then pointed the gun at Big James, "And you, other big dude…..lay across him with hands pointed toward the kitchen. Form an X on my muthafucking floor."

Tim called Tina fearful for the worst. "Tina, what the fuck? This should be over by now. Ya feel me? Where the fuck are y'all?" Tina stared toward the direction of Jasper's apartment. She saw no movement nor heard any noise. She thought about how Jasper had fought Tim and wondered if he took out both of the guys in his apartment. She wondered if anyone was hurt.

She decided to walk toward the apartment to get a better idea of what was going on. Her last words to Tim were, "Leave the car in ten minutes and walk over here if I don't call you back." After she hung up, she started to walk slowly toward the apartment that she once shared with Jasper. She was shaking as she proceeded and stopped when she got near his car. She had thoughts of running to the getaway car and leaving the area with Tim. She knew that something had to have gone terribly wrong considering that she hadn't seen or heard the other two guys, and the silence was terribly eerie. She pulled out her phone to call Big James, but never got to dial the number

She ducked as a Honda Civic drove up and parked. She saw a woman that she didn't recognize jump out and run up the stairs. Tina remained unseen, but her panic escalated even more as Sonya ran to the apartment and hesitated before she twisted the doorknob. She attempted to be stealth as she crept closer, not caring how crazy she looked at that point. She paused just in time to see Sonya push open the door that still had Jasper's key dangling in it.

Jasper almost shot Sonya when the door creaked as it opened. His shock almost presented an opportunity for the two masked guys to start moving. "Whoa! It is just me. What the hell is going on?" Sonya was looking somewhat plain, yet beautiful, as she was still wearing pajama pants, house shoes, and a pink head scarf. Jasper was still at a loss for words. She moved to stand behind him and the gun that he was pointing at the two men squirming on the floor, as she continued, "I would've changed but your homeboy called me saying that some guy named Tim was going to rob you, and that you weren't answering your phone. He begged me to come over and check on you. It looks like you got things handled here."

Jasper pulled up a chair and sat down. He tried to put the story together in his head, but he couldn't. He kept the gun pointed at the masked men and instructed Sonya to call the police. Skeelo moved to shift the weight of the guy lying on top of him. "You two take your masks off....slow and at the same time." He kept the gun on Skeelo since he was most likely to make a move. She walked back into the living room with Jasper's phone and called 911. He asked Skeelo, "Big dude, why did y'all try to rob me? Why is Tim getting you two to do it?"

He recognized Big James right away, but couldn't recall his name. He figured that Skeelo went to Pembrook as well. He assumed that Tim paid them to either rob him or attack him and make it look like a robbery. Sonya grabbed Skeelo's knife and grabbed another chair to sit next to Jasper. Neither man gave their name, while they told the story as they knew it. Skeelo remained mostly silent giving only yes and no answers without any more detail. The look on his face exuberated rage. Jasper ejected one of the bullets from the handgun and tossed it toward the two men lying on the ground. "If you think this is a joke, take a chance at getting hit with one of those."

James started speaking first about how one of his sorority sisters that he barely knew called him crying saying that her ex-boyfriend had slapped her around and that Tim came to the rescue, but he was beat up when he tried to stop the fight. Jasper laughed as he heard that part. James' cell phone rang constantly as he sniffled through his recollection. The two sitting in the chairs sat in confusing silence as Skeelo moaned and begged to get James off of him. Fear was undeniably gripping Big James as he constantly tried to beg for forgiveness. A gunshot wound or the possibility of jail petrified him compared to his partner who only muttered fearlessly, like he was done wrong.

Skeelo was extremely angry at his partner for telling all the details, keeping nothing silent. "You ol' snitch ass bitch! You telling this punk everything!" Jasper had more questions but wasn't sure of what to say next. Sonya wasn't foreign to robberies, guns, and knives as she experienced much as a singer in various bands, but what she was hearing had her amazed. She felt sorry for Jasper and could see the pain he was feeling in his face. She was sitting next to a hurt man, still dressed for church, wielding a gun as he was trying to figure out what he did wrong to deserve what he was going through.

Sonya proceeded to ask the questions that Jasper's racing mind couldn't put together at that moment. James continued to tell about how much Tina was paying them, as well as, how Tim and Tina probably had left them hanging after not reporting back. "Man, I tell ya…..anything you wanna know, man. Me and Skeelo are just minor actors in this. You wanna go after them, man."

Skeelo winced when he heard his nickname said aloud, and by the look on Jasper's face, it rang a bell of recognition. He didn't recognize the faces, but he recalled Rodney talking about his frat brother Skeelo coming in town once. Skeelo spat to his cohort, "Damn nigga! You just gonna tell this dude my name and shit? James. Yeah nigga. Let's put your name out there, too." Jasper foolishly dropped his head, mentally trying to wrap his mind around an attempt to hurt him with an all-Pembrook cast of characters.

James figured that his way out of the situation that turned bad was to tell Jasper enough to anger him in letting them go in order to focus on the orchestrators of the scheme, Tina and Tim. In his attempt to do that, he accidently spoke his partner's name. The realization of what had transpired made his body stiffen suddenly in shock and regret. That gave ample opportunity for Skeelo to push the dead weight of James from on top of him and take an irrational last resort move.

Sonya saw the quick and powerful kick from Skeelo that rolled James over. Before she could scream, Skeelo was on his knees and then his feet. He stood there testing whether he would get shot or not as Jasper raised the gun. "You ain't got it in ya, nigga!" Jasper frowned up deeply as he waited for Skeelo to move again. Little did the bodybuilder in all black know, Jasper had no issue pulling the trigger, and he had enough witnesses to say that he was justified in doing so.

Skeelo moved slightly to look at the door. Jasper replied silently with a change of expression as if saying, *I wish you would.* Skeelo was calculating his chances of getting shot. He was looking for a way to get out of the apartment. He looked around for anything to duck behind, anything to throw, and anything to serve as a distraction. He smirked as he found something, and said, "You little punk ass ni…" Just then, the unlocked front door was opened by Tina.

James' face was pointed to the ground, but everyone else in the room looked and was actually stunned to see her. Tina yelped as she saw the very vascular arm of Jasper's holding a gun. Then she regarded the rest of the room, but focused her gaze on Sonya. "Oh, is this the new bitch?"

"No, you are just the old bitch." Seeing that she was unarmed, Sonya pointed the knife at her and said, "Now close the door and join the party." Tina complied and raised her hands as she walked backwards to the kitchen table and took a seat. Sonya kept the blade of the knife in her hand inches away from Tina's face. Their facial exchanges spoke their own conversation. As Sonya backed up to where Jasper was standing, his gaze not moving from Skeelo, she questioned "Where are the cops?"

At that point, Tina went belligerent. "Jasper, you called the cops? Let them go, and let's talk about this." Sonya answered for her part-time lover in a bold, high pitch tone, "Uh...no, bitch. These two told us everything, and it is too late. Where is what's his name? Tim?"

Tim had anxiously broken what he was told to do and left his position. He drove the car slowly past the apartment building in time to see Tina walking up the stairs. He freaked out upon seeing that. He hadn't heard from anyone in minutes and felt like leaving the scene more than ever. The contents in his stomach were shifting as he held back nausea. He made up in his mind that he would try to call Tina again in a few minutes to see if she answered. If she didn't, he was going to leave, so he told himself.

He moved the car slowly to a nearby spot and parked, but he kept the engine running. He noticed that his hands were shaking, and he felt wet with sweat soaking his black clothing. He kept his eyes moving constantly between the general location of Jasper's apartment and the clock on his car stereo. "Hey Love" by the Delfonics was playing on the radio at a low volume, but Tim didn't really hear it.

Tim sat there looking back and forth and beating the steering wheel of his brother's car. *Man, how did this happen?*

Why the fuck I had to fuck with crazy ass Tina? All the pussy out there and I had to go after Jasper's girl. She ain't that cute. Not for this shit. He wondered what the two other guys were going through. No one came out of the apartment, and he internally debated going in to join the others. He imagined all of the worst case scenarios. *Could they be in there hurt? I wonder if they squealed like a fucking pig. I bet Tina is up there, all crying and shit.* He remembered how Jasper had put the hurt on him and thought, *Naw, it's no way that Jasper fucked those two big dudes up.*

He felt that he had sat in the car for several minutes, but only a few had passed. The feeling of his stupidity and lust over a woman that never really belonged to him intensified his sick sensation. He looked at the clock which read 11:49. He said aloud, "Ok, Ok. I will call Tina and James one more time before I leave." He closed his eyes in hopes of easing his sensation. He prayed for forgiveness and asked for a miracle to allow him to walk away from the situation with no jail time.

Tim wasn't the only one sitting in a vehicle praying. Jeffrey Hooks had just shown up and sat in his vehicle doing the same, though his prayer was quite different. He prayed that his only child was safe and just asleep in his bed. He prayed that he was just lying in bed with a beautiful woman that kept him too busy to answer his phone. He prayed that his gun was sitting in a box or bag and not the cause of life being loss. He prayed that he wouldn't have to visit his child in jail or even worse, identify his body at a morgue or crime scene.

He opened his eyes and rubbed the 9mm in his right jacket pocket. He got out of his car and saw Jasper's still parked. He cupped his hands around his eyes to look inside for a clue of anything suspicious. Then he proceeded to make his ways up the stairs. He reached in his left jacket pocket to get the spare key that Jasper had only recently given to his parents.

On the inside of the apartment, Tina stood up during her tirade to Jasper. She cried fearful, yet angry tears as she looked at James still lying on the kitchen floor with his hands outstretched in surrender. Skeelo's eyes stayed locked in a daring staring contest with Jasper. Hitting the table, Tina screamed, "Baby, I was just mad at how you treated me. Put the gun away before someone gets hurt." Sonya mumbled something and was met with a verbal lashing from Tina.

"You got a lot of balls talking shit to someone who would cut you for talking shit. Just move bitch! I will gut you and stab you in both titties twice before you say 'Ouch'." Sonya seemed more enraged than Skeelo and Jasper.

As Sonya was squaring off verbally with Tina, Jasper was asking Skeelo to sit down. "Bruh, don't do anything stupid. You ran up in here and tried to play me for weak. Jail got some room for ya, but you ain't going to make it if you take another step". The argument between the two ladies got too loud for Jasper to bear, so he screamed, "Both of y'all, shut the fuck up!"

In the time Jasper looked away to say that, Skeelo ducked and lunged toward Tina. He grabbed her by the waist and pushed her toward Jasper with a lot of force. Jasper jumped backed without thinking as he saw Skeelo move. He fired off a shot towards Skeelo which loudly whizzed by Tina's ear as she was sprawling toward him and missed Skeelo by inches. James screamed a thunderous, "Shit!", which drowned out the screams of the two ladies.

Skeelo, focused only on getting outside, heard the roar of the gun as it was shot and continued running toward the door. Once he got outside, he almost screamed himself as he saw the older version of Jasper draw a gun on him and point it toward his head. "Boy, get your ass on that wall. I ain't going to miss!" Jasper popped out two seconds later to see Skeelo looking bewildered. He saw his dad staring at the big guy with murderous intensity, and the magnitude of it all thumped Jasper's spirit enough for him to break down. He dropped to his knees, in tears, still wielding the gun.

"Boy, get up! Go and call the cops. I got this scared, steroid-pumping punk muthafucka. You go call the cops." He then spoke to Skeelo, who was moving slowly toward the wall and had lost the urge to fight and run, "I don't know what the fuck is going on, but I should shoot you just for making me get out of my bed on a Sunday." He clenched his teeth and spoke through them venomously as he continued, "See boy, I am the crazy one. My son...would have let you live and rot in jail. Me...I would rot in jail for shooting you in the dick then putting the hot muzzle of this here gun in my hand slowly up your ass. Then I would put the shitty barrel up your fucking nose and send your brains to heaven for judgment, before your soul had a chance to make it. You...don't...fuck... with my family." Skeelo eyes widened as he listened to the sadistic old man. He complied with no further resistance especially after what he just heard.

Jasper suddenly remembered Sonya alone in the apartment with two people and ran inside. He found James balled up in a corner crying. He then looked to his right and saw Sonya pinning Tina to the couch with a hand around her throat and the knife close to one of her eyeballs. "Shut up bitch! Stop that crying. It's too late to cry now. You called me a bitch? No, you had a good man here, and you fucked it up." Sonya was tough, and Jasper liked that about her. He stood there looking at the show. "You had a good man, with a heart of gold, but you chose to break it." She started crying as she said those last words, and it made Tina start crying uncontrollably.

Chapter 25

At least three or four other neighbors had called the cops after hearing the gunshot. A few neighbors nosily opened up their doors. Mr. Hooks screamed at them, "Call the cops! I got this! Call the cops!" A small crowd amassed in the parking lot. From where they were standing, they could only see an older man pointing a gun at a younger man that was over twice his size. The younger man was made to lie down after a few minutes.

No one had an idea what was going on inside the apartment, nor did anyone venture close enough to find out. They could only speculate what brought about what they were seeing on the hot summer Sunday afternoon. The crime rate was increasing in Memphis, but not many incidents occurred in that neighborhood. The crowd looked on with fear as well as excitement.

Ten minutes after Jasper first saw his dad aiming a gun at Skeelo, two police cars showed up. Two gentlemen got out of the first car and dealt with the crowd. Two more policemen got out of the second and walked slowly toward the area of interest. Mr.

Hooks was relieved to see them inching toward him, but they had their guns drawn. Growing up in the midst of the civil rights movement in the 60s, he had plenty of knowledge on how to address them.

He didn't move his gun off of Skeelo as he shouted, "Good afternoon fellas. I am Jeffrey Hooks. Please stay calm and listen to me. I will gladly put this gun down. I ask that you walk toward me slowly and listen to me. This man and his friend tried to hurt my son, who is there in that apartment. No one is hurt, and there are two women and two other guys in the apartment, my son and the other hoodlum. As you come up the stairs, I will lower my gun, and get down on the ground slowly to keep this one from running or making any sudden movements." Skeelo continued to lay motionless as Mr. Hooks spoke.

The cops kept their guns pointed at Mr. Hooks as they started to walk up the stairs. "Ok, thanks for trusting me. I am going to instruct my son to tell everyone inside to lie down and get ready for you to enter. Please do not shoot. Again, I will gladly lower my weapon slowly as you continue to walk up the stairs." He saw Jasper coming out of the door, and he quickly said to him, "Boy, go back in there, and tell everyone to get on the ground. Put the gun on the table. The cops will come in there to handle them."

Jasper felt fear for his dad's safety as he barely saw the police lights flashing against the walls of the apartment breezeway. He went in and told James to stay still. He then instructed Sonya to put the knife on the dining room table and lay next to the couch. He barked at Tina, "And you don't move." Tina caught his eyes and saw the utter disgust he felt. She did hurt him and would have to forever deal with that, but she never imagined everything would spiral out of control like it did.

Mr. Hooks looked toward the stairs and saw that one of the other policemen was joining the two coming up the stairs. "Boy, tell me that the coast is clear in there." He screamed to Jasper, scared that the patience of the men coming toward him was fading. Jasper looked up, and said "Yeah dad. We are straight in here." With that, the patriarch did as he promised and lowered the gun and placed his hands on the ground away from it. As he continued to lower himself, he looked up to the face of the first of the three men and said sincerely, "Thank you for being professional, sir."

The first cop was a bald black man in his mid-thirties. He nodded at the man who addressed him. He understood where the older man was coming from and took a chance that he was being honest since the look in his eyes showed respect, fear, and integrity. He then hollered at the rest in the apartment as the other two cops handled Skeelo and Jasper's dad. "Alright, I am Officer Waters. All of you in there listen close to me. Do exactly as I say, and no one will get hurt. I am going to ask you all to say your full name one at a time. Then we are going to come in there and slowly pull you all out. Ok?"

Jasper answered for them all. "Ok. There are four of us in here. I am Jasper Hooks."

He looked at Sonya, and she followed, "I'm Sonya Lauryn Mosely."

Tina quickly followed with, "Tina Jackson."

There was a pause for a minute. The cop yelled in there, "Ok, y'all said that there were four people in there." He had asked them to say there name so he could get an idea of where they were in the apartment before he and the others rushed in.

Jasper looked toward the kitchen, and said in a whisper to James, "Come on, man."

James was still crying and sniffled out a weak, "I'm sorry. My name is James." Then he resumed his sobbing. Despite the stress of the situation, Jasper couldn't stifle a laugh. The policemen outside had a hard time controlling their laughter as well.

Two policemen swarmed inside to access and diffuse the situation, while one stayed outside to oversee the two men handcuffed there. They found everyone that spoke and cleared the apartment to ensure no one else was there. As part of the typical police procedure, they handcuffed everyone inside until they could figure out what happened.

Officer Waters separated everyone based on what he saw. He allowed Jasper to sit on his bed as they bagged up the two guns and knife as evidence. Eventually, his father was allowed to sit in the room with him. Sonya told her version of the story in the living room as she sat on Jasper's couch. He instantly put Tina, Skeelo (whose real name was Quincy Robinson), and Big James (whose real name was James Burton) into the police cars. Tina sat in the back of one, while the other two sat in another one.

The ordeal was draining for all involved as they told their perspectives of what happened. Big James left no room for the other two in black to lie, as he told everything and pleaded to make a deal with the cops to avoid jail. He truly didn't foresee things going as bad as they had. He kept saying over and over again, "Mr. Officer, you got to believe me." There was no toughness behind his large, muscular exterior. Skeelo, on the other hand, played tough as long as he could, but he threw some fictitious points in to put more emphasis on Tina. He figured that she got them into the mess, so she had to go down the hardest.

Sonya was allowed to leave once she gave her account. She spoke to Jasper for a few minutes to comfort him. He was frazzled by all the events and hurt beyond her understanding. She hugged him firmly and whispered in his ear. "I say this with the upmost righteous intentions. If you need company…just to be around you…not the intimate stuff, call me. I will sleep on the couch. If you want to just talk, call me." Jasper smiled weakly and kissed her cheek. After shaking his dad's hand, she started to leave. Mr. Hooks called out to her, "Thank you for being there for Jasper." He walked up to her and hugged her as if she were his daughter.

Tina didn't crack under the pressure of being interrogated by the cops. Her face showed spite and annoyance. Once she said, "I want to call my father and speak to a lawyer", Officer Waters instructed for her to be placed back in the car and taken to the nearest station for booking. Jasper's dad managed to slip past everyone at the scene and walked up to the car that Tina was in before it took off. He stared, feeling absolute anguish and mystification for the one that he almost called daughter-in-law. She felt his presence outside of the car, and choose not to look back at him.

A minute later, the car started to move away from the scene. The crowd had thinned out as the afternoon crept on. Tina looked back out of the rear windshield and saw Mr. Hooks still standing there. She saw the disappointment in his face, and he saw the insensibility in hers in that brief second. He stood there and closed his eyes again, raised his hands, and said another silent prayer. He asked for Jasper's recovery after being smitten with such an obnoxious young lady. He asked for compassion against the lost soul sitting in the backseat of the squad car moving away. Lastly, he prayed for the youth of a generation much different from his time.

Tina sat handcuffed in the back of the car unable to cry anymore. Though she was unable to shed anymore tears, she felt true sorrow as she looked at Jasper's father. Her plan of revenge went totally awry and affected many others that she did not want to be hurt. For that, she felt pained. Then just as fast as sorrow entered her heart, it left with the thought, *They chose to get involved. They could have said no.* On the way out of the apartment complex, the police car passed by the location where Tim had originally parked the car, and she sucked her teeth as she saw that it was gone.

The policemen wrapped up the crime scene and saw no reason not to let Jasper stay at his own place. The crowd totally dissipated, the two men in black were hauled off to jail, and the police tape blocking off the scene was taken down and discarded.

The incident was over, and those around as witnesses were getting back to their lives with something extra to talk about that night.

Officer Waters looked at Jasper still sitting in the same place on his bed. He could have passed as his younger brother. He left a couple of business cards and instructed him that he might have to come to the police station for further questioning later in the week. "Young man, you went through a lot today. I don't know what to say, but everything is going to be ok. Things could have been worse." After that, Mr. Hooks spoke with him shortly and walked him out.

Mr. Hooks went to pick up some food for his son and called his wife. He told her that he would fill her in on everything when he got home. He was deeply concerned for his son and begged him to come home with him as they ate. Jasper refused. Internally, Jeffrey Hooks had a million questions about what happened, whether he would get his guns back, and where Tim was, among other things. He knew that he would get his answers in time. He looked at his son and thought about the man that he had become. He was proud of his strength and the bravery that he showed considering the ordeal that he just went through. He hugged his son five times before leaving and looked back twice before closing and locking the door behind him.

Jasper spoke to Shelia to ask for a few days off of work. He was in no mood to listen to Rick's antics. Rodney and Kyle spoke with Mr. Hooks off and on during the ordeal, and Jasper finally called them back. They shared briefly what they heard and knew. Rodney offered to come to Memphis, but Jasper told him not to. Sonya sent a text message with a final offer to come over and some words of encouragement. Jasper didn't reply back.

Hours later, Jasper's parents were watching the news which showed a three minute blurb about the incident and the arrests in Cordova. No names were given in the story, but Officer Waters was shown briefly by the main entrance of the apartment complex explaining a little of what transpired. As his mom watched, she commented that it is sad that a man so young has to learn about hate and heartbreak at such an age. "It ain't right, Jeffrey. It ain't right."

Mr. Hooks responded to his wife while holding back tears. "Through heartbreak comes experience, and this experience is going to make him stronger. He is a Hooks man." Daddy Hooks' right eye dropped a few tears for his son, knowing that he would be ok and thanking God again that the situation wasn't worse. He did tell his wife what happened, but he left out a few details. He vowed to never tell his wife about the gun that Jasper took from the house. He only told her about the 9mm that he took with him.

He had a feeling that Mr. Jackson would call soon, apologetic and embarrassed once the smoke cleared. He had no notion of worrying about that right then as he held his wife tight on their back patio as the sun went down and he allowed a few more tears to drop.

Jasper sat in his apartment still contemplating the events from earlier. He contemplated how he could have ever loved someone so evil. He contemplated whether or not it was his fault that all these things transpired. He felt bad for Tina. He questioned whether brotherhood was truly a part of fraternity as he wondered what happened to Tim. If it wasn't for DeMarcus's phone call to Kyle warning him of what was about to happen, he could only imagine what would have gone down, who would have been hurt, and whether he would have been sitting there on his couch instead of dead or in jail.

He wanted to make a drink, but he was out of liquor and beer. He was too emotionally weak to physically move from where he was sitting and run to the corner store to pick up something. Time lost its sense of value. It seemed that it took forever for the minutes on his clock to change, but the sun seemed to be already setting. He turned on the TV so there would be some noise in the apartment.

A conversation his father once had with him rang true in his head. *"Boy, never let someone hurt you twice. It stings when they hurt you that first time. I know it does, but you can't go on sulking over that damn loss. You hear me, boy? They got you all sad and shit, but you know what….they go on living their life and they ain't thinking about you, while you all sad and losing sleep. They won against you once, and don't you dare let them win again by keeping you down. You hear me?"*

One wonders if they were really in love once it is over. New anger and hatred can make you wonder if you were only lost in infatuation, but the feeling after the sadness and self-pity goes away really is love, and it hurts…at least for a while. It would take a minute, but Jasper knew that he would be ok. After texting Kyle to say that he was ok and sending one to his dad saying thanks, he turned off the phone and got lost in his thoughts until he fell asleep still sitting back on his couch.

Epilogue

Tim raced back to his brother's house once the police cars showed up. His brother came home from playing basketball and saw his younger sibling sitting on his living room floor drunk. He was shocked as Tim told him everything from start to finish. The lies about borrowing the car, the affair with Tina and the botched robbery attempt. As he talked, he kept drinking. He promised his brother that he wanted to be driven to the police station to be turned in as soon as he finished telling him the story.

His brother listened attentively, but screamed back questions from time to time. "Why this Tina chick? I could have gotten you girls if it was a problem." "Why didn't you just talk to Jasper?" "Man, why did you have to use my car?" Tim answered all of his questions and continued to drink. He figured that he was going to jail and wouldn't be able to get any liquor for a long time. As they finished up their session, there was a knock on the door. Both Tim and his brother knew who was knocking. As his brother opened up the front door, Tim bit into the last of the twelve Krispy Kreme donuts that he had picked up. He didn't resist as he was handcuffed and placed into a patrol car.

Hours after the fiasco in Cordova ended, Tara listened to her voicemail messages. Her knees became weak as she listened to DeMarcus pleading for her to pick up or at least warn Jasper of the impeding danger. She looked at the clock to see that it was past 7p.m. One of the messages said something about the event going down by noon. She kept repeating, "Oh my God, oh my God!" as she called DeMarcus hoping to hear that Tim changed his mind.

DeMarcus was sitting on his couch watching the local Arkansas news when Tara called. It didn't matter that they once were lovers or that they really weren't on speaking terms. He answered the phone as if they were friends since childhood. "Hey Tara. How are you? Jasper is fine if that is what you were wondering." Tara felt woozy as DeMarcus told her some of what he knew prior to the incident and what Rodney had told him after the incident. Shame for not picking up the phone and possibly preventing everything from happening plagued her.

"Oh my God, DeMarcus! I am so…" As she began what would have been a sincere apology and peace offering to remain friends, DeMarcus interrupted her and said, "Turn your TV on to channel 12 now." Tara turned on the TV in her room in time to see Pembrook's president speak on what had happened in Tennessee hours earlier.

"The tragic event that happened on the other side of the Mississippi involving former Pembrook students was brought to my attention. I don't understand the gravity of why it happened, but I pray for the young man's safety and state of mind at this time. He is in my prayers, and I ask that you pray for him as well. I cannot intelligently speak on all that happened, but what I heard is an embarrassment to all Pembrook alumni everywhere. I hope all of allegations are not true. Thank you." After that, the President walked away from view of the camera. Tara wondered if he actually cared about Jasper and what happened, and why he even was asked to make a comment.

After a few minutes of awkward conversation, the two ended the call. It was not the time to discuss what had went wrong between them; it was time to be there for a friend. Later that night, Tara hesitated before calling Jasper. After two rings, her ex-boyfriend answered his phone, "Hello."

Rick requested a transfer to another department before Jasper came back to work. He enjoyed the days off and found much needed clarity. He was granted to be a part of the Research and Development department of InfoTech Solutions by the end of the month. He felt that a change of scenery was important to his growth and stability in the company. He recognized his complacency for advancement and conflicting tendency to want to be in charge of something and people. Jasper was just one of the few people that challenged his leadership and that fueled his conflict.

When Jasper did return to work, the two had lunch and shared stories and laughs about people in the building, new technology trends, and opportunities at InfoTech. "Listen Jap. You are intelligent and a quick learner. One day, you will be running a helpdesk, or better yet, your own IT company." At the end of the month, there was a large sendoff for Rick even though he was just moving to a lab two floors down.

The detective handling the case of Jasper versus the conspirators all sitting in jail was livid when Jasper sat in his office and calmly stated that he didn't want to press further charges against all involved other than what was going to come for their crimes. After several attempts to convince him otherwise, Jasper didn't budge on his stance. He only wanted his father to get the guns back, and he wanted to move on with his life.

"Son, are you sure you don't want to reconsider? I know that you aren't thinking about taking (he looked down at his notes) Ms. Jackson back. Are you? At least get a restraining order against her in case she makes bail." The detective wasn't satisfied with just shutting the case down so easily. Jasper agreed to a restraining order and walked out of the room shortly thereafter. After a long talk with his parents, Jasper felt that all of those involved would get what they deserved one way or another. Honestly, he felt sorry for all of them.

Detective Wyrick still wasn't going to let all of those involved walk away that easily. He convinced the apartment owners to press various charges other than the obvious felonies that occurred on the four that dressed in black that day. He said, "That little stunt they pulled may have long lasting effects on the economy of your property. We can't let them get away with that, can we? We can't let young kids think that it is cool to rob good people as they get ready for church, can we?"

Overall, the presiding judge went easy on all of them since no one was injured and the robbery attempt ultimately failed. James, Tim, Skeelo, and Tina all were indicted on various charges and received various amounts of jail time and probation. James received the least due to his cooperation and his minimal involvement compared to the others. Skeelo's knife got him extra months in jail and a longer probation period. There was no strong counter to his claim that the knife was only to instill fear during the robbery and was not to be used for deadly purposes. There was no proof that money had or would have changed hands as payment for the job since Tina denied it. The three of them never spoke again.

Tim received a sentence of 6 months in jail along with a probation sentence of two years. His sentence was lighter since he had no knowledge of the knife nor actually entered the apartment. Discussions about leaving the crime scene and conspiracy convinced the judge that he would need to be punished for the poorly executed scheme. The judge joked during the trial, "Mr. Powell, next time get your own girlfriend. It may go better that way."

Tina angered the judge with her smugness during her time in the courtroom. Her fate was 18 months in jail, along with a recommendation for professional counseling for a year and 2 years of probation. Her parents were there to support her, but were not sitting together. Betrayed by the deceit and lack of communication between them, Mr. Jackson separated from his wife upon hearing more details after Tina's arrest.

Tina was thankful that her punishment was not more extensive, but she was saddened by the sight of her father sitting several feet away from her mother as she wiped away tears of guilt. Ms. Jackson never intended for her daughter to go as far as she did, but she felt slightly responsible since the idea of winning Jasper back was hers. She would never admit that she regretted the pressure that she placed on Tina about her job search and fiscal support.

A week after Tina had her last day in court, Mr. Jackson sat on the couch of the corporate hotel suite he was staying in and called Mr. Hooks. He braced himself for all kinds of curse words and crazy remarks, but he was met with kind words and an apologetic voice.

Ironically, Mr. Hooks was cleaning his two guns after they were released at the end of the investigation. He recognized the number as the phone rang and had a vivid flashback of what he experienced on that Sunday afternoon. The anger in his mind ceased as he recalled the look on Tina's face as the police car drove her off to jail. He answered the phone civilly, "How are you doing, Terrence?" He heard the hesitation in the responder's voice and noticed that it was laced with emotion and alcohol.

Terrence Jackson swallowed hard and replied, "You know that we try so hard to be there for them, raise them right, and love them like nothing else matters. Where did I go wrong, Jeff?"

Mr. Hooks rubbed the graying hairs on his chin and with sincerity said, "You know there, Terry…sometimes we as parents beat ourselves up when our children don't act perfectly. If you measure your parenting against perfection, you will always fall short, because there is not such a thing. What matters is that you did the best you could, because some parents don't even try."

It was always painful for Mr. Hooks to listen to another man uncontrollably cry, but he listened with patience as Mr. Jackson lost it for a minute or so. "I am sooo sorry about what my daughter did to your son. I pray for your forgiveness, and I ask that you pray for us." The fathers talked for hours until Mr. Jackson felt much better. The two fathers would never be the best of friends, but their bond wasn't broken by tragedy

Kyle Scott came to Memphis after graduation from,his leadership course to visit his old roommates, Jasper Hooks and Rodney Kirkland, as well as, visit Pembrook College before his departure to Fort Stewart. Many nights were spent drinking and reminiscing on their pasts, while looking forward to their bright futures.

They attended one of Rodney's shows at Jo Jo's and celebrated the new direction of the band. Still named Dipped in Soul, Rodney had become the band's leader after such a short time of being a part of it. Under his leadership, the group's popularity blossomed making the club's and Rodney's income much larger. It was evident how well liked they were as fans sent the band members, as well as Kyle and Jasper, drink after drink in the VIP section that night.

Dipped in Soul became known in the Mid-South area as "Funk Fusion Pioneers" after a front page article in the entertainment section of *The Commercial Appeal* newspaper highlighted them. The article described how no other band "better fused new school music with their original old school influences" as they were known to play newer songs and transition into the songs in which they were sampled from and vice-versa.

The trip to Pembrook College almost didn't happen. After the traumatic experience that he went through, Jasper found it hard to step on the campus that educated the same people who tried to rob and damage him. Since Kyle was soon to deploy to Iraq, Jasper decided to go along. They hung out on the schoolyard with friends in school as the fall semester had recently started. The three were inseparable until Kyle disappeared for a few hours. It was suspected that he went to visit an old flame for a goodbye gift.

The three roommates and even took a picture in front of the house where their friendship cultivated. Who would have thought that three very different men, that were members of three different fraternities would bond the way that they did? If the walls inside the little three bedroom house could talk, stories of good time and hard times, tragedies and triumphs, wild parties and nights of praying among other things would fill the ears of anyone willing to listen.

As they left to go their separate ways on the last day of Kyle's trip, the sadness emotionally punched him. The uncertainty that war brought made him really look at what was important to him. Several Army manuals and presentations that he saw during his training spoke about always watching the back of those close to you in battle. Well, he knew that the two men that he had grown to know and love would always have his back, and he would always have theirs.

Shelia started to back off on the time that she spent with Jasper. They stayed professional at work and no one, other than Rick, suspected any inappropriateness between them. She made Jasper promise for a rendezvous every so often. Her R's rolled as she said one night, "You will be hard to replace. I don't think that anyone can really give me the dick like that. Our secret, right?"

Jasper could not totally walk away from such a gift horse. He was in a situation to be able to get outstanding sex and professional development at the same time. If he was older, or if Shelia was younger, he might have really given a relationship with her a chance. The fact that they worked in the same building squashed any serious talk of the subject.

On the other hand, Sonya impressed Jasper during the incident in his apartment. They started spending more time together, doing activities in and out of the bedroom. Their differences would eventually cause them to drift apart, and they both knew that it would. For the time being, they were going to enjoy the ride.

For the most part, Jasper was a single man. He walked the fine line between enjoying the freedom that came with that status and overindulgence. Those close to him knew that his heart would sooner or later heal enough to allow another chance at love.

Acknowledgements

Dante D. Long would like to thank:

First and foremost, I would like to thank my two beautiful children for you were the motivation for every hustle and success that I have ever had since you were both born.

Next, I would like to thank the two other "Men of 1302". Your personalities and our experiences in college inspired some of the characters, this book, and the whole series to come. I love you both of you brothers.

I have to give a special thank you to everyone who had a hand in making this dream of becoming an author come true, no matter how big or small. Each and every phone call, proofreading, motivational word, honest feedback, and idea that I got from all of you is much appreciated. I apologize for not naming each person on this page, but there are so many that helped to make this possible. Your support all these years means so much to me.

I have to give a special shout out to all of the authors and others in the publishing industry that ever gave consultation, advice, and kind words. Lastly, I have to say a separate thank you to my editors.

Dark Diamond Publishing, LLC.

Check us out and follow us at

www.darkdiamondbooks.com
www.facebook.com/DarkDiamondPublishing
www.twitter.com/dd_publishing

Read excerpts and subscribe to the newsletter. Stay tuned to future developments from Dante D. Long and Dark Diamond Publishing

Dante D. Long

www.facebook.com/authordante.long
www.twitter.com/authordantelong

About Dante D. Long

Dante D. Long is a native of Georgia and currently residing in Virginia. *When Good Men Go Bad* is his debut novel and the first of the *Men of 1302* series. He is also currently working on various projects.

Learn more about Dante D. Long at
www.darkdiamondbooks.com/author_dante.html